To Cotton ...
here in 98
I am our Author'
Thank you (RM)

THE
STORM
IS OVER

Rosalyn

RARA MASTERSON

2021

ISBN 978-1-64349-632-0 (paperback)
ISBN 978-1-64349-633-7 (digital)

Christian Faith Publishing, Inc.
832 Park Avenue
Meadville, PA 16335
www.christianfaithpublishing.com

Printed in the United States of America

FOREWORD

I don't know if you believe that life's events are the result of coincidences or serendipity or the work of God, but for me, there is no such thing as coincidence. I believe that God is actively working in each of our lives. I read a wonderful book *A Wink from God* by Squire Rushnell. Squire Rushnell describes how God gives us winks or nudges in life to help us make the best of what we are given. He puts people in touch with each other to help them become all they are meant to be. Sometimes those winks are obvious, and others are the most unlikely connections one might ever imagine. This book is the result of several of those unlikely, unimaginable strings of winks from God. It is a story of hope, courage, perseverance, and love. It reveals how alive and well God is in our lives today. It demonstrates how God lifts all of us up to amazing levels of achievement and genuine goodness, especially when we open our own eyes to the many winks God gives us.

This is Rara's story. It is co-authored by Rara, my son Jamey, and myself. A more unlikely trio you would never meet, but it is the result of delicate and improbable threads of human connections is Godly winks stays the same.

I met Rara in 2004 at a Fourth of July picnic at City Park in Denver, Colorado. I was a newly retired teacher looking for new avenues to give my life purpose. My good friend, and as Rara loves to call her "Earth Angel," works at a place called Empowerment. Empowerment is a sanctuary in downtown Denver for women coming from the often-unspeakable walks of life. Empowerment's mission is "to provide education, employment assistance, health, housing referrals and support services to women who are in disadvantaged positions due to incarceration, poverty, homelessness, HIV/AIDS infection or involvement in the criminal justice system. Their goal is to decrease rate of recidivism by providing case management, support services, basic skill education, housing and resource coordination that can offer viable alternatives to habits and choices that may lead to criminal behaviors." At Empowerment, all are welcome.

Earth Angel's job at Empowerment is to help women acquire their GEDs. The women have failed graduating from high school for numerous reasons but are now hoping to achieve that elusive diploma which will help open employment opportunities to them. I volunteer in the GED arena, tutoring the women as I am needed.

On this summery day, I accompanied Earth Angel and several women to the park to help serve the Empowerment women a Fourth of July feast. I met many of the Empowerment participants and their children. The Empowerment staff served up the best of foods, making all feel warmly welcomed and appreciated. Rara was smiling, boisterous, and outgoing to make sure all that came through her food line had enough for themselves and their accompanying children. She laughed and cajoled the various women into taking plenty of everything. She was energy abound!

Earth Angel introduced us, and Rara gave me a big hug, thanking me for helping with the celebration. That bear hug was the first of many I would receive from Rara. I had no idea we were both being winked at by God!

As I spent more time volunteering at Empowerment, my friendship with all at this sanctuary developed. However, I was at a loss for understanding much of what I encountered as I am a product of middle-class white suburbia. The threads of this woven story begin to come together as a result of a book which I received as a gift from a friend. When my friend learned of my latest venture of working with the women at Empowerment, she gave me this book about a woman's life in the inner-city ghetto. She thought it might help a white girl like me to better understand the women I was meeting at Empowerment. The book was a huge help, and I passed it along to Earth Angel. From Earth Angel, the book made its way into Rara's hands, and thus our story begins!

Rara's life and my life began to converge on a course which we never dreamed of. As I recall, the words Rara said to me on that serendipitous day were "that girl in the book ain't got nothin' on my life!" Over time, I began to hear Rara's story, and I knew it had to be told. However, it takes lots of trust and confidence to share life events of this magnitude. The trust slowly developed as a result of more winks and nudges. Rara and I guessed that the off-duty Jefferson County deputy, who found her when she had been left for dead, may well have been my brother. We will never know for sure as my brother passed away months earlier from brain melanoma. My husband and his group of critical-care doctors very likely cared for her as she fought for her life in the intensive care unit since they were the doctors who run the units at the hospital where Rara was taken. Rara finally said that she had the story, but she felt she could not write it. I told her of my son, Jamey, who is a wonderful writer, and I felt he would be willing to do the honors to pen her story with her.

Finally, it was the courage and faith on Rara's part that she was willing to share her incredible story with Earth Angel, Jamey, and myself so it could be written for others. Rara said if her story would allow even one woman who has had her similar experiences to avoid the pain and suffering she has endured, it would be worth the risk to put herself and her story out there for others to read. This is Rara's story. The most courageous woman I have never met.

—Bobbie Heit

PREFACE

My name is Rara, and this is my story. Today I have a job as a crack-cocaine counselor which allows me to serve others and, hopefully, to make a difference in their lives. I own my home, and I have a great car, a green Honda Accord. All these may not sound like much to many people, but for me, this is huge as I never dreamed my life would be so blessed with such abundance.

I grew up in the inner city of Denver, Colorado, and I still live there today. My past is ever present with me, and it nearly destroyed me. The family should be our source of comfort, hope, direction, and purpose. My family, in truth, was one of destruction, neglect, abuse, and despair. Even now as I have tried to break the cycle of drug and alcohol abuse, many family members continue to sabotage my efforts, judge me harshly, and see me as arrogant. They do not understand that I wish for a new way of life for my daughter and myself.

Most of my life has been spent trying to please others, listen to others, and do as others have told me to do. I hear rewound tapes going nonstop in my head reminding me those who should have loved me but instead saw me as stupid, ugly, fat, lazy, unvalued, and completely incapable of doing anything with my life. Those ongoing destructive messages cost me much in life, including the loss of my eighteen-year old son to suicide. Because I valued myself so little, I allowed myself to be abused and developed both an alcohol and crack-cocaine drug addiction. Those addictions nearly took my life one late September night in 1996.

In my search for love and belonging, both family members and scores of men repeatedly abused me physically, sexually, and emotionally. Love and acceptance for me was never freely given. I was bought time and time again for alcohol and drugs. After accepting the "loving gift" of alcohol, my body was given over and over to one-night stands and all sorts of attacks and abuses.

Since I never had any reason to value myself, I never thought I deserved anyone of value in my own life. I am working at seeing myself as a beautiful woman capable of any dream I dare to dream. I am a certified addiction counselor who longs to save others from the horrors I have experienced in my own life. I am trying to help my beautiful twenty-one-year-old daughter to complete her education and lead a drug- and alcohol-free life. I want her to be truly loved and valued by those important people in her life. I am journeying to the place where I can believe that I don't have to settle for food from the garbage can but can dine at the table with Denzel Washington.

What a dream and what a daily struggle it is to get there. My hope is that this book will bring my life peace and healing. My other main goal in writing this book is to give other women, who find themselves in the deep, black hole of drug and alcohol addiction, the hope and courage to survive and lead the abundantly good life God wishes for each of us. It is terribly difficult to dig out of those awful holes, but it can be done, slowly, one day at a time.

It has taken tremendous courage and huge balls for me to come forward and share my story. It has been a terribly painful and often-times an agonizing journey in reliving my story in order to get it down on paper. There have been those who doubted that I could write my story, those who thought I was not capable or strong enough to get the job done, but after two long years, it is done, and I did it!

The past can haunt you, but for me, my past is my power. I have learned that with God I am safe. I have become tuned into the daily winks I receive from God. He has given me those who care and the courage to listen to those who have intervened in my life so that these words could be put down on paper. This is a mission I have been called to do in hopes that my story will empower other women to find strength from their past as well.

A gift is a gift is a gift. A gift that is given with genuine uncon-ditional love is the best gift to receive. I have been given so many gifts over the past ten years. I have met many earthly angels who have given of themselves freely and openly to me. My Earth Angel greets me daily as I enter Empowerment to do my work. She embraces me with such love and acceptance that I find myself floating over to her work space often during the day just so her wings can keep me afloat, especially when I wonder if I am doing a good job. What I find is that I am often able to give to her the gift of experience; I have discovered that I have gifts to offer to others too. Sometimes the Earth Angel doesn't see how our participants are taking her for a ride as she lacks my street experience; this is something I have plenty of! We give gifts to each other daily, and that is truly a remarkable joy for me.

I have so many people I wish to thank who have given me gifts. You will meet many in my book, but there are numerous others who have given to me unconditionally and have given me so many more chances than I deserve. There were those who listened to me speak the first time I shared my testimony. They showed me the power of my past; they encouraged me on this journey long before it even began. When I was done speaking, I received a standing ovation from those people, many whom I did not know. Me! It has taken me many more years to have the courage to complete this project. I have reached deep inside to go forward with this book even when it became too difficult to reach back and relive all that I have experienced. I learned to walk through my fears, to face my fears head-on, and to know that I am still okay.

This is my story. I hope it brings all who read it courage, hope, and a deep faith in God. This is what I have gained from living my life. This is my story and told to the best of my ability as true as I remember it to be. This is my reality, and I realize that other friends, acquaintances, and family members may disagree with what I have written. But this is my story as lived and experienced by me. All names of those whom are still living have been changed in an effort to protect their identities. To all the women who are still broken vessels, I have been one too. I have come out on the other side of drug-and-alcohol addictions as a stronger, better, more hopeful person. My wish for all those who are still broken is to be brave, take courage, and break those destructive addiction cycles. With God, all is possible.

2848 RACE STREET

I can see that big ol' ass mansion; it never goes away. Someday, I don't know why, but someday I want to own that ol' house. I guess it is really not a mansion, but when I was little, it sure felt that way. It was the only home I ever knew. That house haunts me; that house nearly destroyed me. I can remember times when it protected me and gave me comfort, but there were few of those safe, happy memories. Those were the times when Big Daddy was alive. After my grandfather passed, that house dealt me neglect, abandonment, and abuse.

It was a huge house, at least in my mind. From the outside, it could cause envy to all who saw it. It was a three-story house with a porch which wrapped around the front. Awnings enclosed the front windows to help keep the hot afternoon sun from cooking the inside of the house. One of my most favorite spots was the swing in which I would curl up on Big Daddy's lap and listen to him tell me stories or sing me his songs. Big Daddy took lots of pride in the front yard. I remember a beautiful leafy tree that we helped him plant for the whole neighborhood to admire and enjoy. He loved that tree, so did I. A tall green hedge kept much of the house from view of the neighbors, although everybody knew everybody on Race Street. That hedge hid the horrors that took place behind those innocent-looking, closed doors.

The 2848 Race Street was a fine house. The sitting room and living room were the hosts to many of Nanny's dignified churchgoing lady friends. As Nanny was a deaconess in her church, it was her responsibility and delight to host the women after Sunday services. She would set out her pretty dishes, cups, and saucers on the dining-room table. Big Daddy always dressed in his nice shirt and slacks for Nanny's friends, but he didn't go to church, and he preferred to stay outside with the kids rather than mingle with Nanny's church friends. Nanny shooed everyone out of the house so she could enjoy tea with those women; my grandfather chose to be outside in the backyard keeping a watchful eye over all of us. He wouldn't say much about those women other than to call them "Clara Mae's friends." He'd pray like Nanny but not as loud or as long. All he needed to do was to thank God for His blessings at night before he climbed into bed.

Amazing smells wafted from the kitchen. The whole neighborhood knew when there was cooking goin' on in that kitchen. Both Nanny and Big Daddy could cook! Chicken and dumplings, beans and ham hocks, sweet potato pies, you name it; it came out of the kitchen. Nanny's dinner rolls would have put Betty Crocker and Pillsbury out of business! I learned to cook in that kitchen, and I make a mean fried chicken.

Every Sunday was the gathering day of our family. My aunties, uncles, and cousins came for favorite meals. Dinner was always served at five to five thirty in the afternoon; it was never late. Big Daddy always sat at the head of the table; he was the family protector, the family peacemaker. The few happy memories I have of that ol' house came from those family gatherings. There was laughter, storytelling, and a sense of belonging during those precious days when Big Daddy sat at the head of that dining-room table. He was a quiet sort of man, not much to say, but everybody knew when he was upset. What Big Daddy said, went. I always remember the house being Nanny's house, but Big Daddy ruled the house, sometimes with an iron fist. As long as he was there, peace, safety, and calm reigned in our home. There was no arguing between Nanny and Big Daddy; they waltzed with each other through their lives, each tending to the business which was theirs to tend to. Nanny was the disciplinarian, and Big Daddy was the children's protector. As long as Big Daddy was there, Nanny was not able to dish out her whippings on the kids. Actually, nobody got whippings from anybody if Big Daddy was there.

At any given time, a number of family members lived at 2848 Race Street. Three bedrooms occupied the second floor. Stairs curved up from the entryway to the bedrooms. I hated those damn stairs as I swept them more times than I can remember and always by hand as we did not own a vacuum. Of course, Big Daddy and Nanny occupied the biggest bedroom at the top of the stairs. Directly across the hall from their bedroom was the second room which was claimed by my older brother, Andre, and my cousin Snake. A bathroom and linen closet were found as one went farther down the hall. I loved that bathroom with its tiled floor and big claw-foot bathtub! Finally, the last bedroom was shared by me; my mother, if she happened to be with us at the time; my sister, Caspar; and Nanny and Big Daddy's adopted granddaughter, Cece. Why all we girls had to be shoved into one little bitty room, I don't know, but that just was the way it was. The hallway was big enough for a rollaway when an extra bed was needed. We were the mainstays of 2848 Race Street, but it was not uncommon to have other cousins, aunties, or uncles come to stay for a while. Seemed like if anybody needed a place to stay, they'd always ended up at Nanny's house. Some folks seemed more welcomed than others; Andre and I were always at the bottom of the guest list! And when there were others who came just for dinner or for an extended stay, we regulars got put to the side. They came first; we didn't count for much.

A back porch overlooked the backyard. It was a rickety, shaky porch with no screens on the window frames or door to help keep all the flies out. Big Daddy bought Nanny a modern washing machine which was kept on the porch. When the wash was done, she hung it on the clothesline in no time. Big Daddy did some "remodeling" of that porch; he added a sink and a toilet to keep the washing machine company. He put walls around the sink and toilet for privacy, but the walls were so thin that it felt like you did your thing out there on the porch in front of God and everybody. Seemed like anyone or anything could just march on up to that of porch and come on in. I was scared of that porch. After Big Daddy passed, more than once I was cornered and trapped by the sink and toilet by various members of my family for beatings. I remember one time when my mama and Ursula held me down while Andre beat the shit out of me. I couldn't escape. Nope, I didn't like that porch!

The backyard was nothing special; little or no grass grew there. Big Daddy kept his chickens in the backyard too. He loved his chickens as they made for great eating! He'd use to pick one up when it was time, wring its neck, strip it clean, and there was dinner! An old Chevy car took up space in the backyard along with the chickens and clothesline. Nobody could see what went on back there. I know I was pretty damn confident that nobody seemed to care about what was back there or what went on in this dilapidated space as I found my mama smoking my weed in that old car. She had found my first lid of weed, and instead of confronting me about smoking pot or telling me I shouldn't, she smoked it herself! She then informed me that if I could afford to buy marijuana, I could have it. That's all she had to say to me as she smoked my pot. I couldn't believe it! I was thirteen years old.

A scary basement existed in 2848 Race Street. A side door on the outside of the house led down to the basement. It was unfinished and spooky. An old piano lived down there but little else. Nobody liked to go down there as our house was mouse and roach infested, particularly the basement. It was damp and forever dusty. During one of my return stays at 2848 Race Street, my uncle told me that my son and I could live there in the basement if I cleaned it up. Clean it I did! I got rid of all the junk, old clothes, and boxes that were down there. I wanted to make it as my own, and I took pride in cleaning up that old basement for me and my baby son, Coco. One can learn to live with mice and roaches if it means having a roof over one's head. I offered to pay $100 per month to live there; my uncle took me up on my proposal, and I did indeed pay him $100 per month rent for that roach and mice infested hole. No other family member who lived in that house ever had to pay rent, but I did.

The 2848 Race Street was Nanny's house, and she let everyone know it. Big Daddy let her be the owner, but he was the boss. I suppose I should be grateful to Nanny for letting me live there as, more than once, I was reminded that there was no place else for me to go. Nanny never threw any of us out of her house; her door was always open. It would be years later that I came to appreciate what Nanny and Big Daddy did for my brother and me. If we had not had them, we would have ended up God knows where.

Nanny was a tough old girl who was very particular about her house. Once Big Daddy was gone, I became the Cinderella of the house. I had to clean and clean and clean. It seemed to me that I was the only one who ever cleaned Nanny's house, not my mother, not Cece, not Caspar, and heaven forbid that any of the menfolk ever helped. When Nanny said, "Jump," I'd jump as high and as fast as I could. I was there to serve all those people around me, cleaning up after them and doing whatever Nanny wished. At the time, I guess I figured that was just how life was. Why my mother or Cece or Caspar or anyone else was never asked to do things, and why they didn't get beat with extension cords, I don't know. I always wondered why I was the only one who cleaned! Mama was supposedly grown, and as an adult, she was never asked to do anything. Besides, no one ever knew if she was going to turn up on any given day. Nanny always had a special feeling toward Cece, and that girl was lazy, so she never did anything. Caspar was my little sister, and she would get scared of Nanny and run to hide. I think I did her share of the work to protect her from getting beat. Rara do this; Rara do that. If ever I questioned Nanny why I was the only one who ever had to clean, and question I did, the extension cords or switches came out. My Nanny would stand over me and beat me with those cords or switches. Cowering down and covering my head, I tried to protect myself. When it got especially bad, I would run for it. My dear sweet family members, whether it was my mother, my brother, or cousins, they would catch me and hold me down until Nanny was finished teaching me a lesson about talking back. I think the beatings were Nanny's way of making sure I didn't turn out like my mother, or maybe it was because she had been jealous of my Big Daddy loving me the way he did. I'll never know except that once Big Daddy passed on, I received more than my fair share of whippings. I went from being a twelve-year-old happy little girl to becoming the Cinderella of that house.

There were dark secrets that lurked in that mansion. Abuses happened to me that never should have happened, and nobody knew my dark secrets. Adults were doing their adult activities while children played their games, out of sight from their busy caretakers. My brother Andre did things to Caspar and me that nobody ever knew. He said we were just playing house, and I needed to do what he said. He explored my body; he touched me and raped me a couple of times. Because of Andre using my body for his own pleasure, I never valued my body as a sacred place, a place which was not to be violated or toyed with. I told no one, not even Big Daddy, what took place upstairs at 2848 Race Street. Would anyone believe me? Early on I learned that my body, my very being was not my own. It was to be enjoyed by whoever demanded acts of me, and I had no right to say no. My self-worth was zero from the time I was a little girl. Because I didn't value myself as a person who had the right to be loved and protected from a very early age, I thought I never deserved anyone who would truly care for me. My poor choice in men goes back to these secretive, destructive sessions. If my own family did not respect me as a girl or as a woman, how could I possibly expect anyone else to treat me as I deserved to be treated? Those playing-house sessions created dark and dangerous destructive anger in my heart and soul. I would find a way to take care of Andre, one way or another. As for Caspar, she ran away from home at the tender age of fourteen and did not return for nearly twenty-four years.

With abuse from Andre going on, I guess I didn't ever feel very protected from others, even family or friends. When I was twelve, my cousin Zoey was married to a man named Lyle. He was her second husband and a pedophile. Lyle managed to sexually assault both Caspar and me. We didn't tell anybody. Those dark, ugly secrets just kept piling up in my heart, and nobody ever knew.

My mother and daddy were never around or interested in being my parents, so Big Daddy and Nanny raised me. I can remember a horrific experience when I was all of nine years old. Nanny was at church, and my mother was at the Bingo hall hustling money. Andre was constantly pestering me; he was relentless. He never left me alone. On this day, I was peeling potatoes with one of Nanny's knives, a particularly sharp knife and one she used on only special occasions. Andre came into the kitchen and would not go away and leave me to do my work. Before I even knew what happened, I ran up behind

Andre and stabbed him in the back of the thigh with that knife. My dark anger had erupted from the depths of my soul. I could not take one more crushing comment or touch from this relentless brother of mine. As he lay in a pool of blood, I can remember being so frightened and scared that I ran screaming to hide behind Big Daddy in his rocking chair. I thought I had killed my brother. Ursula came running in and found Andre. That girl slapped the shit out of me, trying to calm me down. Big Daddy quietly sent Ursula to get our neighbor Miss Alma. Miss Alma wrapped his leg in a towel while Ursula called an ambulance. Once Andre was rushed to the Children's Hospital, the police were called. Big Daddy told the police there had just been an accident in our home. He took me into his arms and soothed me. Not once did he yell or scream. He kindly explained to me that it had been an accident and that everything was going to be okay. I believed him and truly felt it was an accident because how could I have ever done something so awful to my own brother. I knew deep in my heart of hearts that I had wanted to hurt Andre for all the trauma he had caused me in my life. Nobody understood how a nine-year-old girl could have done such an act against her brother. Nobody knew what my brother had done to me. My grandfather forgave me and protected me from the others who were so anxious to harm me. Because of the attack, I had to appear in juvenile court. My mama went with me to the hearing; had I been older than nine, my mother would have asked the courts to take me away and preferably never allowed me to return. However, at age nine, charges cannot be filed. From that time forward, my mama had only eyes for Andre; I was a troublemaker and could do no right. I was blamed for everything Andre did, and she constantly tried to find ways to dispose of me. I would remain safe from my family's anger, abuse, and neglect as long as Big Daddy was alive. That fateful day that Big Daddy went to the corner store and never returned, my life became a living hell.

The day Big Daddy died of his heart attack, 2848 Race Street was very quiet. Everyone was solemn about the funeral arrangements. Since Nanny was a deaconess in her church, Big Daddy had quite a big send-off. He would have never needed all that hoopla for his good-bye, but I think it helped Nanny. She never cried in front of us, but I can remember hearing sobs from behind her closed bedroom door. Nanny never remarried after Big Daddy died.

With Big Daddy gone, there was nobody left to protect me on 2848 Race Street. Nobody checked Nanny from her tirades which resulted in my numerous beatings. My mother encouraged my brother Andre to take over the father role now, and he, too, found multiple occasions to beat me. Most of the scars on my body are the results of my brother's need to teach me lessons. He would beat me with extension cords, hoses, slap me across my face, and call me names like whore or bitch. My mother didn't care what happened to me. The more beatings I received, the better! My understanding of how family works, plays, and loves became skewed as I had no viable role model left. From this time forward, the only lessons I learned about family relationships were how to use, abuse, neglect, and abandon those who are supposed to care for you the most. There was no longer any kindness, compassion, laughter, or love at 2848 Race Street. It was the beginning of a lifetime of self-survival; I had to take care of me as best I could because nobody else would. I played the role of Cinderella for 2848 Race Street for the next several years, always trying to find a way to escape the brutality. Unfortunately, every time I would discover a way to be free of that ol' mansion, my life would be turned upside down by my family members, and I would find myself back there again.

After Big Daddy died, 2848 Race Street was never again my home or my refuge. It was only a place where I knew pain, abuse, neglect, and abandonment. As Nanny got older, she lost control of her house to Andre and Snake. Andre became a heroin/cocaine addict while Snake evolved into an alcoholic. When they were under the influence of alcohol and/or drugs, those two grown men became mean and uncontrollable. Nanny stayed out of their way as best she could. Nanny's house had always been a refuge for her adult children and grandchildren. As drinking and drugging were prevalent on the property, the police were often called to come to quail the raucousness or violence which erupted all too often. Tiny, elderly Nanny would often find herself between bickering adults trying to bring peace once more to her home. Every Saturday, the uncles would visit Nanny and 2848 Race Street to see how Nanny was managing. After all the residents at Nanny's house had a big Christmas party in December 1982, my uncles and aunt decided that the house was no longer safe for Nanny or anyone else. They decided it was best for everyone if they moved Nanny out and sold the house. Andre raised his hand against my uncle while he was coming off a drug-induced high. This episode escalated the uncles' desire to follow through on the house sale. For the first time ever, the family scattered to various places in Denver. Nanny was shuffled from house to house living a little with each of my uncles and my aunt Stella. This was the safe haven provided for my grandmother. Finally, after all her family was evicted from the Race Street home which she and Big Daddy had always tried to provide to their ailing family, Nanny ended up in a nursing home. That broke her heart and her spirit. She had lost her dearly beloved home and family. Clara Mae died twenty years after Big Daddy. Once 2848 Race Street was sold, the physical domain of my early abuse was gone, but the scars it left would haunt me forever.

BIG DADDY

I have one, and only one, person in my life who ever really cared about me as a human being. My maternal grandfather, Big Daddy, Edward Franklin. He loved me and cared about what happened to me and guided me. As long as Big Daddy was close by, I was safe; he was my protector.

I lived most of my early life with Big Daddy and my grandmother, Nanny. My mother was too busy hustling and gambling to care for my brother Andre or me. Our daddy spent most of his time in jail. Big Daddy never minded caring for me. He would hold me on his lap for long periods of time, and nobody, I mean nobody, could pry me from those big strong arms.

When I was a little girl, I remember being happy and feeling secure. Even though neither of my parents raised me nor cared much about what happened to me, I don't remember feeling unloved or not wanted. I always had a place to call home. Big Daddy made me feel special, important, and treasured. I was his baby girl, his little "Ham-Hock Legs."

Big Daddy was a big man; he was about six feet one inch tall and weighed nearly three hundred pounds and was big boned. His beautiful, big, brown eyes were always dancing with a song or laughter. His toothless smile was as wide as the sunshine and could light up the darkest day. I can't help but to smile and laugh when I see his smiling face in my mind; it didn't seem to bother him that there were no teeth in his mouth. That wonderful smile! Not a hair could be found on his bald head or his soft kind face. Best of all was Big Daddy's big, wide Indian nose, my nose. I had Big Daddy's nose!

His voice was deep but could be thunderous. His hands were huge like the size of a football. They were strong, working hands, and when his hands enveloped me, I always felt so safe and warm. He had a huge ol' rocking chair in the living room. He'd lift me into his lap, hold me close, and rock me. He sang to me and called me his "Little Sista" or "Little Ham-Hock Legs" or "Baby Girl." I knew I was special when those huge hands held me close to his comfortable blue overalls. My Big Daddy always wore a plaid shirt and blue-striped denim overalls with huge, hard-toed, combat boots. Big Daddy would fall asleep with me on his lap with his arms wrapped around me as though I was a soft, squishy teddy bear. Other folks were not allowed to hold me when Big Daddy was around; I was his precious bundle. Everyone else was jealous of Big Daddy's special relationship with me, including Nanny.

He kept a can of snuff in his right-side pocket and was always chewing. He never drank, smoked, or drugged; he just chewed snuff. Snuff was his only addiction. Alcohol was called "firewater" by Big Daddy, and he would have nothing to do with it. I don't ever remember seeing my grandfather drunk, ever. I wonder how the head of the Franklin household was never a drinking man when the rest of his family was poisoned by it.

Big Daddy worked for the railroad for thirty-five years; he was among the first black men to work the daily train between Denver to Winter Park. As a railroad brakeman, he was proud to provide well for his family. My grandparents lived in Globeville before Big Daddy bought 2848 Race Street. Globeville was an area of Denver near the railroad tracks. Railroad work was hard work, and Big Daddy worked long hours. Both Big Daddy and Nanny saved their money as best they could; in many ways, they were both penny pinchers. However, the most amazing memory for me about my grandparents' finances is that Big Daddy bought a brand-new fancy car every year he could afford a new one. Neither he nor Nanny drove, but they had themselves a fancy car to go places in. Other family members gladly assumed the role of the family chauffer just so they could drive the new car. Aunt Sista was the first driver, later followed by Stella.

Whoever did the chauffeuring took Big Daddy to and from work, to pay his bills, grocery shop, and wherever else he may wish to go. Driving the car came with responsibilities; no free ride there! The family chauffer could never be late in picking up Big Daddy from work or not be available for his errands. If you drove the car, you did Big Daddy's errands first.

Big Daddy was a soft-spoken, gentle man. He never had much to say. I remember him always smiling, humming, singing, or telling stories as he walked around the house. My Big Daddy was like a gentle giant. But when he would get upset, his deep, thunderous voice would roar "Clara Mae!", and that would be it. Clara Mae was his name for my Nanny. My grandparents really never fought; they each seemed to have an understanding of whose job was whose in the household. They allowed each person to be as they were meant to be, and nothing ever needed to be said about who the other had become. Nanny could have her church ladies over to the house for afternoon tea, but she best never expected Big Daddy to stick around to hear those old biddies talk about their church committees or gossip.

Family took care of family, and Big Daddy loved his family, all of us. He was the protector and center of all the kids' lives. My mama was his youngest, and he always had a soft heart toward her; maybe that is why she never had to accept responsibility for her own poor life choices. If Big Daddy or Nanny ever corrected her or reprimanded her for her crazy lifestyle, I never witnessed it. When Stella, my mama's sister, said mean things about my mother, Big Daddy would not hear it. He also never ran Stella into the ground for marrying a "wife beater" or having five kids by three different fathers. Big Daddy loved his oldest daughter, Sista, in a very special way. On more than one occasion, he would take me and Andre downtown to rescue her from the bars in Five Points; he never once criticized her or berated her for her drunken behavior. He would just say she had a problem drinking her firewater. I was Auntie Sista's namesake, and Big Daddy called me "Little Sista." Sista died young from alcohol disease, and a part of Big Daddy died as well; he was never the same after her death.

Big Daddy had high hopes for his grandson Snake. He loved Snake as his own son and encouraged him in all his dreams. Snake was a tremendous basketball player, and Big Daddy loved to watch him play. When Snake graduated from high school and won a basketball scholarship to a college in Baton Rouge, Louisiana, my Big Daddy was so proud. He bought Snake a car, a pink Thunderbird! My cousin's college career was short-lived as he began experimenting with alcohol or firewater as Big Daddy called it. Big Daddy never gave up on Snake even when he dropped out of school and ended up killing his best friend in a car accident. My grandfather forgave him. He tried to help Snake forgive himself for that awful accident, but Snake never did let go. Snake lost his dreams forever; drugs and alcohol destroyed his promising life.

Big Daddy believed in the best of people. He never felt anyone to be a lost cause. Big Daddy tried to get my daddy to be a daddy. A serious discussion occurred more than once with Daddy about how he needed to change his life, stop being foolish, and raise his kids. Big Daddy informed my daddy that his life made no sense, and he needed to make something of himself. Of course, my daddy never took Big Daddy's advice. My daddy ended up in prison serving time for burglary on three different occasions.

My grandfather also never allowed anyone to hurt his family. My mama's second man, Ox, beat her up one time too many. Big Daddy marched over to Ox's house and told him that if ever he laid another hand on my mother, he'd be back to kill him. That's how we came to live in Nanny's house in the first place. After Big Daddy stood up to Ox, Mama, Andre, and I moved to our grandparents' house. And when my aunts and uncles told my Nanny to let the state take me and Andre away from 2848 Race Street because our mama and daddy didn't want us no more, Big Daddy stepped in and thundered "No!" As long as Big Daddy was around, I knew I had a home, and I was safe. My grandfather was available to me when my parents were not. He never let anything happen to me. He was all I had.

One fateful Sunday morning, my life changed forever. Big Daddy walked down to the corner store where he had his own account set up. As he neared the corner, he fell and died instantly of a heart attack. I was too young to understand; all I knew was that my Big Daddy went to the store and never came back. He had broken his promise.

When he died that awful day, I was only twelve years old. I lost the only one who truly loved and cared about me. I lost my only life's mentor. Big Daddy had left me. When you are little and someone promises you that they will never leave you, you believe them. Big Daddy promised me he'd never leave me, and I trusted him. He was the only one I ever trusted. However, life often deals us an unexpected hand of cards, and you have no choice but to play that hand.

Big Daddy was gone, and I had no one to protect or love me from that day forward. I sometimes wonder how my life might have turned out if Big Daddy had not died when I was so young. The nightmares that made up my life for the next thirty-five years might never have occurred, and I might have turned out very differently. Kindness, gentleness, compassion, forgiveness, and love were the legacy my grandfather passed onto me. He was the only one who truly loved me for who I was, and he protected me. Big Daddy was the only one who ever asked me how my day at school went or what I had learned that day. He would tell me I was smart and capable of doing well in school. He believed in me. It has been said that those who care for you in your earliest years imprint you with special characteristics for life. If it had not been for Big Daddy's imprinting on my soul, I think I would have lost my life long ago. Big Daddy taught me what true love was all about; he showed me how to be kind, gentle, and compassionate. He demonstrated that anger did not have to end in violence. People have taken advantage of me all my life because of these traits, but they also saved me. These characteristics have been burned into my soul and became my lifeline, even though they would be buried for endless, sorrowful years.

SWEETS, DADDY, AND THE FRANKLIN CLAN

S weets. Who calls their mother "Sweets"? My mama was one of a kind; God broke the mold after He made her. That's a good thing!

Sweets, Barbara Franklin, her given name, was the baby of the family. Big Daddy and Nanny had five children including Bums Jr., Felix, Geraldine, Stella, and Barbara. In the Franklin family, each person had their own special nickname; a family tradition that originated with the Texas Franklin family, and this tradition is carried on today. Bums became a successful businessman as did Felix. Big Daddy and Nanny were so proud of those boys. Bums married Ramona, and they had four children, Roger, Joanie, Joann, and Dorothy. This family was the model family in that Bums and Ramona stayed married and saw all four of their children through college. They have currently been married sixty-one years!

Felix was married as well and had two children, Felix Jr. and Cece. Despite Felix's financial success, he had destructive personal habits including gambling, wife beating, and womanizing. His wife left him and took her son with her. Felix never thought Cece was his daughter as he was sure his wife had got it on with another man. Cece landed in Nanny's house, and Nanny loved her as her own daughter. Nanny always treated Cece with special love and care.

The Franklin daughters didn't fare as well as the Franklin boys; two of the three girls never finished high school, and all developed addictions of one kind or another.

Sista held a special place in Big Daddy's heart. Sista had two children, Snake and Zoey. Due to Aunt Sista's drinking problem, Snake also became a permanent resident at 2848 Race Street. Zoey got married at fifteen because she was pregnant.

Alcoholism claimed Auntie Sista's life while I was still a little girl; this loss broke Big Daddy's heart. I had been called "Little Sista" until Auntie Sista died; that nickname died with Sista.

Stella produced five children by three different men including Ursula, Eunice, Luke, James, and Patty. Because Stella always held a job and was self-sufficient, she generally thought very highly of herself and judged the rest of us to be far beneath her. However, Stella had her little quirks too. As her children grew up to be high-school age, she managed to move her kids out of her home, and they would slowly make their way into Nanny's house. As Stella's kids moved in, Andre and I were moved aside. They became the "guests" of the home, and we were shoved to the side.

Then finally there was Barbara, Sweets. Big Daddy treasured daughter, but Sweets was the apple of his eye. But she was a bad apple. Sweets, like the rest of the Franklins, was a tall and beautiful lady. Being well dressed and styling was also a Franklin trait, and Sweets was particular of her appearance. The show was what really mattered most to her, and she was a good-looking woman who could attract the best-looking men around.

Sweets met my daddy in high school and married him at sixteen. My daddy was all of eighteen. They began their life together in a little apartment not far from Race Street. Andre arrived in 1957, and I came in 1959. Our little family stayed together a few short years before my daddy was arrested for burglary. Off to prison he went, for the first of three times. My daddy never really took responsibility for his family.

With my daddy in jail, it didn't take long for Sweets to start looking for a new man for herself. Ox was the next man Sweets hooked up with, and like my daddy, he was a good-looking, big man and a wife beater. Sweets popped out five children, one after another, with Ox. My half siblings included Capt'n, Ernest, Caspar, Professor, and Fonze. You'd think a woman having this many children would be interested in being a mother but not Sweets. She was a hustler, only interested in making money and looking good. As for Ox, he couldn't keep his hands off her. Sweets fled to 2848 Race Street after one particularly bad round with Ox. Big Daddy marched over to Ox's house and took care of business. Ox never laid another hand on Sweets again because Big Daddy told him if ever he did, he would kill him. Ox believed him, and thus Andre, Caspar, and I moved into Nanny's house with Sweets where we became permanent residents. My half brothers remained with Ox as both Ox and his mother said no woman would ever take his sons away from him. As for Caspar, well, it didn't matter much seeming how she was a girl. In our world, sons were always more important than daughters.

With all seven of Sweets's kids being looked after by someone else, she became free to do what she did best, hustle money. Sweets was a brainy woman, and she had a few good jobs, but she would rather be looking good, gambling, and drinking to showing up for any job on a regular basis. My mama was a gambler. She'd use whatever money she had to play her game. Fraud was her game; she would hustle bad checks and credit cards. When she was desperate enough, she would send me out to help get a hold of more money. More than once, she gave me a bad check to cash for her. My mama told me if I would hustle for her, I could earn a few extra bucks for myself. When I hustled for her, we were both usually drunk. When we were sober, neither of us ever thought much about what we were doing. I'm not sure if I knew what she was up to at the time; maybe I played her game in hopes of winning her love and approval. The irony of it all is that Sweets never once got picked up by the police for her hustling, but I sure did. My own mother hustled me, and I would fall for her scheme. Who allows her own kids to risk going to jail for her desire for money? My mama did! Her addictions consumed her. Since her children were being raised by others, she could live with Nanny and Big Daddy on an "as need" basis, and all of her earned income and welfare checks went straight to clothes, gambling, and booze.

We were pretty much an inconvenience for her. Sweets always loved Andre, but she couldn't care less about Caspar and me. After all, we were girls. Mothers and sons connected; daughters were a throw-away item. The Franklin family history for its daughters continued. As girls, we were problems who always needed correction;

they wanted us to be good girls; what defined "good girls"? Our brothers could drink, drug, womanize, get in trouble with the law, but we, as girls, better not walk that path.

Someone would beat into us that we were to be good girls, usually Andre. However, all of us girls ended up on that path of drug and alcohol addiction in our search for acceptance, love, and belonging. We had no role model for being "good girls." Nanny didn't count; she only disciplined us severely which turned us away from her. Our mama was no mama, and our aunties were no better.

Sweets always showed up at Race Street after an encounter with her latest man ended in her getting beat up bad or the man just got tired of her and walked out. She came and went as she pleased. She was always promising me and Andre that she was going to get us our own house where we would be a real family, but that never happened.

I, on the other hand, became her whipping child. If anything wasn't going Sweets's way or even if it was, my mama criticized me and called me names. I can hear her calling me those horrible names today; they have been branded into my mind forever.

Those "terms of endearment" like piggy, tramp, crazy, whore, lazy, bitch, ugly, worthless, and stupid were names Sweets called me. I was never far from reminders that I would amount to nothing and was worth even less. She never once hugged me or told me she loved me; never. It is no wonder I clung to Big Daddy and treasured the kind and lovable names that he called me.

I liked school, but back in those days, nobody asked questions. And we never told what went on in the house on Race Street. I guess, in most ways, we didn't know that our house was any different than anybody else's house. But school didn't always like me. We were poor, and other kids, even though they were poor too, made fun of me and Andre. Kids got to pick on kids; Andre and I were great targets. I'll never forget one cold winter's day. Andre had a big furry-type coat that he was so proud of. The other kids always made fun of our clothes and called us names, but Andre loved his coat. As he hung up his coat on the coat hook in the room, a big ol' mouse climbed out of his sleeve. Those kids never let us forget that incident. We were poorer than poor to have mice living in our clothes.

I did do well in school. Some teachers seemed to want to help me, but as I moved through school, few really ever encouraged me to do well or stay in school. It was just a place to meet friends, to make plans, to drink and smoke pot. Looking back, I wished someone had noticed me and help me realize that I was smart and capable of becoming whoever I wanted to be. However, as far as I was concerned, the only voice I ever heard in my head was Sweets's. I had zero self-esteem, no confidence, and no knowledge that I was capable and smart. When I was a little girl, Big Daddy used to tell me I was smart, but his voice had long disappeared from my radar screen. I hooked up with an older guy and got pregnant at fifteen. Sweets encouraged me to have an abortion so I could stay in school. I had the abortion, but by sixteen, I had dropped out of school. I spent my time in bars drinking instead of going to class. I tried an alternative school once after I dropped out of regular high school. A counselor there encouraged me to get my GED, but I was too busy spending time going to the bars and partying. Back in the '70s, they never checked your ID. And besides, I always found older men who were more than willing to buy me booze in exchange for sex.

When I found no love at 2848 Race Street, I turned to neighbors for the affection, love, and sense of belonging. The lady who lived down the street would talk with me, show interest in me, and even hug me. I liked being at her house. But she was the one who first allowed me to get drunk in her house. It was acceptable to do these activities in the presence of the adults; it was considered far safer. Experiment while under an adult's supervision where it can be monitored safely. Go figure; my neighbor who had shown me true acceptance and love when I needed it most, introduced me to my life's addiction, alcohol. Who does that? Of course, Nanny beat me within an inch of my life the first time I came home from the neighbors, drunk at twelve years old. I wondered if she ever told the neighbor she shouldn't let me drink. My Nanny told me I would burn in hell forever for that loose kind of behavior; wonder why she never told that to my mama! Because of the first beating and the raining of God's wrath on my head, I never wanted to have anything to do with God. He was way too scary! And as for my mama, she simply smoked the pot that I had gotten on my own at thirteen. My daddy fixed me a hard liquor drink of Johnny Walker Red whiskey and milk that I drank under his supervision at the "innocent" age of sixteen. At first, drinking and, later, drugging scared me, but I thrived on the effects of alcohol, so I continued. I felt like I belonged when I drank; it empowered me. The more I drank, the more often the whippings would come, mainly from Sweets and Andre. Nanny began to participate less in abusing me.

As time went on and their supervision of me became less, my family couldn't keep up with me. I began to experiment with combining alcohol with marijuana. This was my new way to love, acceptance, and belonging. Andre's best friend, Alvin, had a twin sister, Betty. Betty introduced me to pot. Andre ended up killing Alvin in a car accident while driving. Andre and I drank and smoked pot many a time together. And I had no trouble finding those who would give me drugs; I always had company when I drank. Life was good, or so I thought. I was seeking love in all the wrong places. The alcohol allowed me to attach myself to somebody, anybody, and I belonged.

Andre was always the loved child. He could do no wrong. But when he did do wrong, somehow or another, Sweets would always blame me for what he did. When I was sixteen, Andre set me up for a big fall. We had both been drinking that day. Andre stole a purse. He gave me the stolen credit card to go into a record store to buy him some records. He told me he would buy me some records and some new clothes if I helped him. I thought it was a cool and exciting thing to do. I am a slow learner, and I trusted my brother to be my friend. Stupid me! That day, Andre and I were both sent to jail and then onto juvenile hall. As a matter of fact, Andre, my dad, and I all ended up in jail at the same time. Our father had been arrested again for burglary and was serving another sentence. I know each of our prison numbers: my daddy's number was 00669, Andre's was 58400, and mine was 66900. I wish I had graduation dates to remember instead of prison inmate numbers. As for Sweets, she believed I had caused the trouble for Andre, not the other way around.

By the time I was sixteen, my mother nearly got her wish of doing away with me forever. Sweets was on prescription drugs at this time. She suffered from depression, and she told the state that she could not manage me anymore. She had me committed to the psychiatric ward at university hospital. My mama informed them that I was an out-of-control teenager whom she no longer could handle. I was a drunkard and druggy who needed help, and she could not handle or control me. My mother told them not to send me home as she was too sick to supervise me. Why didn't somebody see who had the real problem? Who had turned me into a drunken alcoholic at sixteen? I spent six weeks on that ward begging for help with my drinking problem. After being treated with Antabuse and Lithium, I went from one group home to another. I eventually ended up in Job Corp for six weeks.

Job Corp was a safe haven for me. There was one counselor there who encouraged me to get my GED at an alternative school, but instead, I found people like me who liked to drink and party. Life was grand! I didn't have to worry about anybody beating me. I was finally free to do as I damned well pleased. I drank and had a good ol' time. I was on the run! I can remember one night, hitchhiking; I wasn't scared of anybody. A car stopped, and these two white guys drove me to Golden. When I refused to have sex with them, they kicked me out of the car, and I had to take a cab back to Denver. I had no money to pay for the ride. My Nanny refused to pay the cab fare, so I went to jail. The fine was $50, and I had to stay in jail until I could pay the fine. Now how was I supposed to do that when I had no money, no job, and nobody, including my family to help me out? One of Sweets's men friends paid my fine. I was feeling grateful to this man for helping me out. I should have thought twice since he was one of Sweets's friends. This man paid my $50 fine, and in return for him taking care of the fine, I decided to go with him to California to help him pick up a van. While in California, he introduced me to lots of his friends, drinking friends. I had a great time. Once we got back to Denver, we stayed at his mother's house. All went well until he began to hold me hostage and beat me. He would supply me with booze and pot and then force me to have sex with him over and over again. I finally decided I couldn't live like that anymore, and I escaped back to Nanny's house. I was back at 2848 Race Street.

My mother continued to find ways to sabotage my life even when she no longer was "responsible" for me. She stole from me. When I was all of nineteen years old, I was pregnant for a second time by the same man. I was determined to have this child; I thought I could have someone all my own and be a good mama. The loser father of my child never cared about me; he just liked getting me drunk for the sex. I worked and managed to save enough money to have my own place for my baby and myself. I wanted so much to raise my baby in a safe, happy place away from all the crazy people who lived on Race Street. I managed to get an apartment of my own to bring my new son home to. While I was in the hospital with my baby son, Sweets came to see him and me. Why I didn't recognize her hustling and manipulative ways that day, I don't know why. Maybe I wanted so much to believe I had finally done something right in Sweets's eyes that I fell for her ploy. She told me she wanted to go to my apartment to bring back some precious clothes in which to bring my son home. I gave her my apartment keys so she could do something nice for a change. That woman, my mother, went to my apartment, ransacked my apartment, and stole the rent money that I had saved. When I was released from the hospital with my son, I had no rent money. I was able to hang onto my place for a few months, but my mother had set me too far back. I was evicted, and with no place to go, I headed back to 2848 Race Street. My own mother had hustled my son and me out of our own place. This was my first eviction, and it was devastating.

Once Coco was born, I tried to become a good mother, but I was surrounded by people who just wanted to party. I needed to get into my own place where I wasn't always partying, drinking, and smoking pot. I found work, saved my money, and moved into my second apartment. I hated being alone. I met an older guy and moved him into my place. Picking good men is not my strength, and this guy was one more loser that I added to my collection. He was a drunkard and a gambler. He gambled away my rent money, attacked me in the middle of the night, stabbing me twice in the arm. He went to jail, and I was faced with returning to Race Street. I just couldn't do it, so I moved in with my cousin Zoey.

Zoey reminded me lots of Sweets in that she liked to party and look good. They both were show pieces at parties and never wanted me around. I embarrassed them, and besides, I was too young to go to their parties. They saw me as fat, ugly, and when I got drunk, they said I was embarrassing to be around. I tried to do my part while living with Zoey. I cleaned and cooked and contributed my part to running of her household. I thought I was doing a good job and not being a freeloader. Zoey had three daughters, and she slept around with different men as much as I did. One night, I brought a man back to my room in her basement. The next day, Zoey threw me out of her home because she said I had not shown her daughters respect because I had had a man sleep in my room. I have always been held and judged by different standards than the rest of the Franklin clan. Since I had no place to go, I returned once again to Race Street.

This round at Nanny's house proved to be difficult as everyone was there. Sweets and her boyfriend, Andre and his girlfriend, Snake, Nanny, Coco, and I all shared Nanny's house. We were a partying clan; we loved to drink, drug, and carry on all day and all night. At this point, Nanny was too old, too tired and had lost all control of her home.

She could not tell any of us no or throw any of us out, so my uncles and aunt did. They sold 2848 Race Street, and for the first time, the family scattered.

I had learned about Section 8 Housing and got my name on the list. This is how I found my place on 20th Avenue. I thought it was only going to be Coco and me finally. However, I didn't turn my back on my mother or brother; I allowed Andre, Sweets, and her boyfriend to move into my place. I was trying to do the right thing. Sweets continued to play cards, the lottery, and the dog races. She loved those dogs. As time went on, Sweets overtook my damn house. I lost control of my own house. There was ongoing partying and drinking just like there had been on Race Street. Sweets's people simply moved the drinking and drugging from one spot to another.

This same scenario reoccurred more than once. I'd moved to a new place, my new beginnings; Sweets and Andre would come too. When I had a place not far from Race Street, Mama and her man,

Don, moved in with me. I had bought a TV for Coco. Andre stole my TV from my little boy and pawned it so he could buy himself more dope. What kind of craziness was I living in that family members do things like that to each other? I lost it! I couldn't live like this anymore. I broke every window out of my place except my and Coco's bedrooms. I wanted those damn people out of my house. I was done. My mother and Andre moved out.

Andre developed a heroin/cocaine addiction. When he got high, he lost control. As time went on, Sweets became scared of her beloved son as his behavior became more and more unpredictable, violent, and volatile. One night, he killed another man over a woman. It happened in the parking lot outside Sweets's place. Sweets gave him to the law as she was afraid they were going to kill him. She told them he was hiding out at Stapleton Airport in the parking garage. Somehow or another, Andre's killing of that man was my fault in her eyes. Andre was sent away to jail for a long time. I was nowhere near her place that night, but she still blamed me. Sweets was indeed a crazy woman, crazy. But for the first time in my life, I was out of Andre's harmful reach!

I made efforts to be a good daughter throughout time. One Mother's Day, I called Sweets to wish her a Happy Mother's Day; Andre and I were both doing time in prison. When she answered the phone, she told me she couldn't talk with me because she was talking with Andre. As always, she had no time for me. She hurt me over and over, but for some reason, this incident cut me to the core. She had always loved Andre more than me. When would I ever learn?

My life with my mother never had any resolution. She continued to try to hurt me whenever and however she could. I took revenge once. I managed to steal $250 from her. I really didn't see it as stealing; I was just paying myself back for all she had taken from me. But, damn, Sweets developed cancer. I was afraid to go to the hospital to see her because I had stolen her money. But I did go. When I went to the hospital to see her hoping to be accepted, forgiven, or loved, she only accused me of stealing her damn money. I denied it to the very end. Sweets died. There was nothing that even resembled a mother-daughter relationship. Nothing. My mother and

I smoked crack cocaine together two weeks before she died. Can you imagine? Sweets passed away, and I was finally free; except, I wasn't free. That woman forever haunts me. At one point during counseling, I was advised to make restitution to my mother for the money I had stolen. Maybe in making up for the $250 I had stolen from Sweets, I could finally find some peace in the failed relationship I had with my mother. Thirteen years after she died, I helped my brother buy a headstone to mark the place where she was laid to rest. I have yet to see the headstone that I helped to purchase, and I still have no peace from Sweets.

My daddy didn't serve me much better although he didn't persecute me the way Sweets did. He simply abandoned my brother and me. When he was released from prison after one of his burglary charges, he and Sweets got together again for a brief time. We all lived together as a family for a short while. But Daddy was a mean man. He beat us and made us stand in the corner for hours on end.

Grandmother Macey wanted to see us and be a part of our lives, so Daddy would take us on Sundays to see her. She taught us about the Bible which was really important to her. Every time religion was presented to us, whether by Nanny or Grandmother Macey, it was generally followed by whippings and harsh words. I loathed religion; it meant only pain and suffering for me. Daddy and Sweets didn't make it long this round either. Daddy was arrested again for burglary. At least, we didn't have to go to Grandmother Macey's again!

When Daddy got released from prison after another round, he found himself a new woman and made a new family. After all, Sweets had moved onto more than one man while he sat in prison. He abandoned Andre and me again. He seemed to care lots more for his new family. He had a new son, James Jr., another half sibling to add to our collection of brothers and sisters. However, Daddy didn't like being responsible for his new family any more than he did his old one. Daddy was arrested again on burglary charges. This time, the judge threw the book at him; he is still serving time. He was charged as being a habitual criminal. He was given thirty-four years and is doing time.

My family is toxic. They have poisoned me my entire life with use, abuse, and abandonment. I never knew love from any family member other than my Big Daddy.

My mother tried to rid herself of me always. My daddy was incapable of being a father. Andre caused me more physical and emotional damage than any other human being in my life, and that is saying something! Caspar ran away at fourteen to escape the abuses we endured. My entire family fed me alcohol and drugs; misery loves company. It was years later while I was in counseling that I came to realize that Nanny was hoping to make something of me. She raised me as best she could. Her beatings and berating were her way of trying to make me different than my mother. Nanny knew I was special to Big Daddy, and she needed to try to make me turn out different for his sake. I can forgive Nanny for abuse because that little woman gave me some life skills I have been able to use and hang onto. She taught me to cook, clean, and work hard. She meant well. No family member other than my Franklin grandparents ever made me feel valuable or loved. Every time I would try to do something positive in my life, they kicked me down, reminded me of how stupid I was and fed my addictions. They continue to do so today.

THE MEN IN MY LIFE

Every woman's life has unique and different experiences. My experiences with men have been anything but good. However, these events have shaped my life for better and worse; the result being that I am a survivor and an independent woman as a result of these relationships.

I have always defined myself as a woman by having a man's pair of shoes under my bed. I have had more men come and go in my life than I would like to admit. Many of them were no more than one-night stands. I woke up many a time not knowing whom I was with, where I was, or how I had gotten there, but I would always manage to get back home. Many of these men were abusive, drunkards, or druggies. My choice in men has rarely been good.

My relationships with men have been highly affected by my lack of good, healthy family male relationships and male role models. With Big Daddy dying so early in my life and my daddy spending most of his time in prison, I had little to go on as far as evaluating what kind of man with whom I would want to spend time. I sought love through men, but they provided me with my alcohol and drugs, rarely love. I wasn't picky; they could be married or not. I never had much of problem spending my weekend with a married man as long as he'd buy me my booze. I had a motto that I lived by: Let's get drunk and fuck. We'd have a good ol' time, get drunk, have sex, and then they would return to their damn wives. I didn't care if they were married or not, as long as they did not beat me; however, rarely did these men not beat me. Maybe I didn't know any better as that is how it had been in my whole life.

Older, dark, and handsome men were the kind I liked. The ones who were tall, handsome, smelled good, and drove a fancy car drew me in so quick and hard that I rarely considered if they were persons of character or not. Older men could also buy me my booze without any problem, so I tended to gravitate toward them. I would always say to myself that I'd rather be an old man's baby than a young man's fool. My first sexual experience was with my brother Andre as I have mentioned before. So I guess I was on the fast track sexually from the very beginning. I believed sex was always accompanied with a bribe of some sort. Andre would forever have some kind of goodie or candy to offer me if I would just do this or that for him. He'd want me to kiss his penis or let him see my vagina. We did have actual intercourse, but he was too young to really have a full-fledged erection. It became a natural course of events for me as I got older to provide sex in exchange for alcohol or drugs.

I've been in round beds, waterbeds, vans, and big trucks, not to mention, cheap motels. I did it all for booze and drugs. I have slept with men for booze whose dicks were too old to use. I did not value myself as a person, as a woman enough not to be used by men. All of these actions were well before the live birth of my son, Coco, at the tender age of nineteen.

I met my son's father, Charles, when I was fourteen. I was babysitting for a friend of my mother. Charles was this woman's sister's man, and he would sometimes come in while I was watching the kids. There were times when he would take me home from the job. Charles was a tall, dark, beautiful man who dressed impeccably, drove a Lincoln Mark IV, and was a womanizer. I flirted with him when he would come onto me; I was flattered that this beautiful man could have eyes for me. The first time I had sex with Charles, I thought I had found my way to heaven and back again! He was the man I wanted to share the rest my life with. I got pregnant by him twice; the first pregnancy ended in abortion. The second ended with my treasured son, Coco. Charles didn't stay around long enough to care for Coco or me. He never physically beat me but raped me many a time. If I told him no, he would still do it to me anyway. Charles was a fucking buddy. He would watch as some of his closest buddies raped me. Sometimes these dudes would bet on who could last longer as they raped me. They bet they would not come before a time period measured by a stopwatch. Sometimes they would just come to pick me up for an orgy, me, a minor and the only young girl at the party.

Charles was forever the man in my life. I wish I could have been his woman. I dreamed it would someday be Charles, Coco, and me. It never happened. He never had any real interest in me; I was his young trophy girlfriend with whom he could do whatever he wished. He'd buy me my booze, have his way with me, give me a few dollars, and be on his way. I just had to be with Charles whenever he came around. Even when I was with other guys, if Charles came to my house, I was his. I could never tell him no. He was my dream man, and I hoped each time he took me that we would end up cherishing each other for the rest of our lives. No matter how much he abused and used me, I clung to my hope for life happily ever after with Charles. One difference between Charles and all the other men I had was that he was a beer and weed man; he didn't go in for the hard liquor like most of the others. Toward the end of our relationship, Charles would say he was going to kidnap Coco and me and take us to live in the country in Arkansas. We'd be a happy little family there where he grew up. It never happened, and besides, I eventually got tired of him using me, forcing himself on me, always wanting to have oral sex. Charles was partial to oral sex, and I never liked it. I tried to move on, but through the next several men, Charles was always in my picture.

I did move onto other men. The more I partied, the more men I had. These men were never interested in me as a person; they only wanted one thing, and I gladly provided it as long as I got booze and/ or drugs. I never prostituted myself for money, only for booze and drugs. I remember this guy, Keith, who was from the island of St. Thomas. I was all of seventeen. He was an ugly dude who liked to do pot instead of alcohol. He smelled like hell. Keith would buy me booze which was his sign for me to take off my clothes. As he bought me my booze and would have his way with me, he would remind me of all the guys I had slept with to get booze. He would say, "Take a number, and I'm just your next number in bed." He belittled me; he simply wanted to remind me of what a worthless human being I was as he too had his way with me.

Sex and abuse went hand in hand for me. If it wasn't the man beating me or attacking me, it was their women. There was once a woman who accused me of flirting with her man. She broke a bottle and cut me across my right cheekbone. To this day, I have fine pieces of glass in my cheek. At the age of twenty-two, an old man cut me in two places on the left arm. I experienced shooting two to three times over sex, booze, and drugs. I contracted gonorrhea twice. The first time, I got it from a guy while I was pregnant with Coco, and the second time from a guy named Timmy. I had a second abortion as the result of guy named Woody. Woody was married but was separated. He didn't want any more "complications" in his life, so he paid for the abortion. If I couldn't have the man, I sure enough didn't want his baby, so the abortion was fine by me. I was partying with sex and booze, and I got burnt. The consequences of my partying life did slow me down a bit as I eventually geared myself toward staying with one guy for longer periods of time rather than the one-night stands I had become accustomed to having. I kept looking for the man who would love me for me and not for what I could give him.

In my search for that love and the man who would provide security for me, I went through many relationships. There were a few who really cared for me, but for most, I was their sex/booze and partying gal. For the next several years, I did only booze. Crack cocaine was not in the picture until my daughter's father came into my life.

Several men come to mind as I reminisce about the men in my life. There was Frank. He was an older guy, a nice guy who drove a Cadillac. He never hit me, and he did try to make an impression on me as a young woman. He told me real women don't act like I was behaving, throwing themselves at any man who came along. He told me to put my liquor away and pull my act together before it was too late. It was good advice; except, Frank advised me of those things as he was walking out my door after he had come to my bed. I could not take him seriously because he was doing to me the same damn thing he was telling me "real women" don't do!

Then there was Chill. He was a friend of my mother, Sweets. So many of these men knew Sweets because she was a gambling woman who got around town. Chill was married, drove a gold Electric 225. And he would come around on the weekends because I was his weekend woman. He wasn't too violent; he'd smack me around, but he never really hurt me. Alcohol and pot were his poisons. The thing I remember most about Chill is that there was nearly a shootout at Nanny's house between Charles and Chill over me! They were fighting over whose car I was going to get in. In the end, I went with Charles, as always, but I think I was thrilled to see those grown men fighting over me!

I met Sherman at Nanny's. His dad was a bootlegger, and Sherman was in the family business. This man was the first guy to buy me things. He would take me shopping and buy me outfits and shoes. I remember he actually bought me a pink baby doll nightie. I had never had anything like it before. It made me feel so feminine and treasured. Sherman was a pushover, and he was scared to death of my brother Andre. For the most part, Sherman had a milder disposition. But I crossed him once and paid for it dearly. I stole some of his bootlegging money; I needed more booze. He confronted me about the theft, and I denied it. We got drunker than skunks, and I told him I wanted to have sex with him and his buddy. In the beginning, he was okay with our little threesome. However, in the end, he decided it made him look weak to share me with his friend, so he decided no threesome. He beat me up to save face. Sherman gave me the worse black eyes I ever received from anyone. I ran home to Nanny's and didn't leave the house for several days. When Sherman came to his senses, he came to Nanny's to apologize to me. I, however, was in the basement entertaining Charles and had no need for any apology. We didn't see each other for a long time. I ran into him eventually at the bus stop and invited him over to my place. I lured him in for a little round of booze and sex. We remained friends over time; I even rented out a bedroom in my house to him. Of course, I was with another man at that time, but that didn't bother Sherman.

After Sherman, came Eric. I thought he was the one who would really care for me. He wanted me just to himself and wasn't willing share me with others; that was a new concept to me! He objected strongly to having any other people around when he came to be with me. Eric wasn't violent; he was a regular sex fiend. I was able to keep him satisfied. During the time I was Eric's woman, he was killed. I never found out what happened to him. Seemed liked anyone who wanted me, just me, they ended up dead in the end.

I next took a liking to a transient named Crazy Frog. He earned his nickname by jumping around like a frog every time he got high on liquor. While hanging out on the streets, I noticed Crazy Frog because he seemed to have an eye for me. Panhandling and drinking were his game. Crazy Frog would work day labor to get his drinking money if panhandling wasn't producing. He moved into my house for nine months. Frog wasn't a bad dude; I just grew tired of him and his crazy ways. He wanted me to move back to North Carolina with him. I had no interest in living there with him and his sister, so he just up and left.

I guess Crazy Frog wasn't crazy enough for me because the next man I hooked up with was Cut Throat. He moved in with me in my house on Lafayette. When Cut Throat drank, he got mean violent. The thing about Cut Throat was that he was a little dude, skinny like a pencil. He beat me up one time too many; he was the first man with whom I became violent. He jumped me one night too many; I got mad and grabbed a bottle. I broke it and came swinging at Cut Throat. I cut him very near his jugular vein and stormed out of the place where we were hanging out. I found myself with Sweets. I can remember her saying that there was no way she would ever let a nigger that size make her face swell up like he had done to me several times. Looking back, whenever anyone beat me, I would always somehow excuse them and end up blaming myself. I always thought I had done something to deserve the beating. Like many times before, I found myself sitting in my house with Cut Throat. He had enough sense to go get himself stitched up. But the attack was reported to the cops. When they came by the next day and found us sitting together on the front porch, Cut Throat did not accuse me of a thing. I was grateful. Shortly after our spat, he moved on.

My next male relationship was short-lived. Birdie wasn't a very big guy, and he had weird lime-green colored eyes. He was just one of the crowd that I hung out with on the streets. This dude was really crazy and controlling. He prided himself on being a pretty boy, but he sure couldn't perform in bed. I hated being with men who couldn't get it up. When Birdie got drunk, he would go crazy. He had some kind of real psychological craziness going on. After being with Birdie for just a few weeks, he let loose and broke the picture windows out of my house. Out of fear, I called my father who had just gotten out of prison. For the first time, my dad helped me get rid of Birdie. My dad even helped me fix my windows.

After that scary situation, I linked up with Suave. Of course, he knew my mother. He was an old dude, and we became friends; he was in his forties, and I was in my twenties. Suave was one sharp dresser, drank expensive liquor, and loved hanging around with young ass. That fine man drove a powder-blue Cadillac. Poor Suave couldn't perform in bed. I was so disappointed. I liked drinking that fine liquor and riding in that beautiful car. Sauve never knew of my disappointment because he was always too drunk to realize he couldn't get it up!

Crazy Kojak was next. He was a boozer and a gambler. That ugly ol' man stole my rent money for gambling, and we ended up being evicted because I had no money to pay the rent. When I confronted Kojak about my money, he attacked me with a knife. He sliced up my left arm real good. Kojak hit me so hard and violently in my breasts that I still have pain there from him until today. He went to jail, and I moved to my cousin Zoey's house because I had lost my rent money once again.

Stanley was a fine, tall, brown-skinned man who smelled so good. I can still see him in my mind today. He was terribly handsome. We met through a mutual friend. He, too, was an older man who drove a Seville. This man was a cook by profession, not a loser who just hung out. I remember Stanley well because I started using cocaine with him. But he stole my Christmas money that I had saved up for Coco. When I confronted him about it, he denied ever taking my money. I had nothing to do with him after that, but

Stanley smelled good, looked good, and dressed sharp from his head to his toes.

My previous boyfriends, Cut Throat and Tommy, were friends, and that's how I met Tommy. Tommy, my daughter's father, introduced me to crack cocaine. Tommy would buy it for us to share. At first, crack cocaine scared me; however, the more Tommy got it for me, the more I liked it. Tommy was a married man and a truck driver, but his wife put him out. He and I struck up a conversation; one thing led to another. He'd show up on the weekend; we'd talk; he'd get me drunk and then have his way with me. But Tommy was one mean dude and was very controlling. He would make me strip down to my birthday suit and beat me with his belt like I was his little girl. After he beat me, we'd have sex, do crack cocaine, and drink. I grew weary of Tommy and tried to set myself free of him. I was scared of him, but when he had no place to go, he'd always show up. We'd get to drinking and doing our crack cocaine, and then he would want to beat me up; we'd be back to where we started. It took me some time to rid myself of Tommy.

The next guy I remember coming into my life was Corey. Corey was an alcoholic, and we would experiment with crack cocaine together. Corey was the first man who showed any interest in me as a person and not for sex. He actually bought me nice things like food, cigarettes, outfits, and shoes. I didn't think I needed any clothes. I never went anywhere, but Corey took good care of me. He stood by my side when others deserted me. He lived with his mother down the street, and when I got tired of him, I just sent him on down the street back to his mother. I did this when I wanted my own way, or I found out his money was all gone. I was the one who introduced him to crack cocaine.

Corey took care of me in spite of how I treated him. He supported me while I was in prison, making sure I had all the money I needed. We'd talk on the phone, and he'd send me whatever I would ask of him.

Corey was a diabetic. When he found out that he had diabetes, he went clean. No more booze or crack cocaine. Corey relapsed. During his relapse, he stopped taking all his medication for his diabetes. He went into a diabetic coma and died. I was in treatment when I found out he had died. I was so upset when I found out; I blamed myself for his death. I had been the one to introduce him to crack cocaine. This dear sweet man who loved me was gone.

Next came Denzel. Denzel was the first man whom I can honestly say really loved me. He would actually sit and talk with me. He wanted to know about me! He protected me from Tommy and Charles. He claimed me to be his woman and would not allow Tommy to even come into my house. It was Denzel who helped me have my last dealings with Charles. He stood up to Charles. Charles came to my house asking me to store his old Riviera in my garage. I didn't have a car, so there was no excuse for me to turn him down, plus it was Charles! Had Denzel not been living with me, I know I would have allowed Charles to not only store his car in my garage but have his way with me as well. But my Denzel, my wonderful, strong Denzel told Charles a flat-out no. He said I was his woman and that he'd simply have to find somewhere else to store his car. No one had ever told somebody else that I was his woman. Denzel cared about me!

Denzel drank, but he didn't like drugs. He hated it when I would do my crack cocaine. He would tell me that I was putting poison into my body. At times, he would physically abuse me but not always. He just would get upset when he'd see me drugging. He couldn't stop me though; I'd sneak around to smoke my dope.

I met Denzel while I was working, but I loved hanging out with him so much that I quit my job. We would work for the temp agency to get money for our booze. Denzel and I also panhandled together. We would sell some of our food stamps so we could buy ourselves booze if we were low on cash. He showed me how to go to different churches to get free food. Life was so free and easy! Denzel was homeless and didn't mind being on the streets; I however sought out a shelter. I didn't like sleeping on the streets, even with Denzel. We had a mutual friend Bruford who was celebrating his birthday. That Saturday, we bought some vodka for Denzel and Bruford, and we went to Bruford's house just to hang out for his birthday. Denzel drank while Bruford and I did crack cocaine. I had to leave to get back to the shelter on time so I would not lose my place there. Denzel started to walk me back to the shelter when he remembered he had left his boots in Bruford's house. He went back for his boots and never came back out. I read in the paper the next day about Denzel's death. The paper said he had been stabbed in the heart and eye and had died. Bruford killed him and was sentenced to twelve years in prison; I would miss Denzel for years to come. Once again, a man who really seemed to love me ended up dead.

I was celibate for the two and one-half years that I was in Cenikor. While at Cenikor, my entire focus was on getting well, clean, and sober. It was all about healing for my family and me. I needed to figure a way to get my kids back; that was my first priority. My mind was really not on men at all. I was trying to deal with all the guilt and shame I carried because of the lousy lifestyle I had chosen. Besides, the thought of men scared me. I didn't know what a clean and sober looked like since I had never known one of that nature other than Big Daddy.

After I left Cenikor, there was a huge Fourth of July family bash at Zoey's house. I met Robert through family at the party. He was a friend of my cousin Johnny and his woman, Frankie. They knew about this man and his past, but they didn't care enough about me and my children to warn me of his ways. Robert seemed like a nice man. He was chubby and had a cute innocent smile; I was drawn to him. Robert told me that he neither drank nor drugged; I noticed that he used neither at the party. I thought maybe I had found a clean, sober, and safe man to hang out with. He was kind enough to take my daughter, Princess, and me home from Zoey's party even though Lakewood was a far drive from my cousin's house. And he asked me for my phone number.

Robert was a chef and made good money. Looking for a change in his life, he had moved to Colorado where he was staying with family. After seeing him for a few weeks, he told me that his family needed him to move out and asked if he could live with me. I asked Coco how he felt about Robert moving in with us. He wasn't too keen on the idea, but Robert would sleep on the couch (only for a short while!) and help us with the bills. Coco thought he was an okay guy and believed him to be clean and sober as well. So as it goes, Robert moved in, and he treated us all very well. He was kind to me, and he'd take me to and from work. It felt good to have a man in my life, especially a clean and sober one who seemed to care about my kids and me.

During this time, Princess was caught playing with matches. She lit a match and burned a two-by-two-inch hole in her bedroom carpet. I let her have it but good. Robert stood by and did not interfere with me disciplining my kids; he didn't think it was his place. However, Robert used this incident with Princess to take advantage of her. It was during Christmas break when I could not afford day care for Princess during the weeks she was out of school. I was spending my extra money on drugs. Robert graciously offered to watch her while I was at work. He worked the night shift, so he was available to care for her during the day. We trusted him; he seemed like he truly cared for all of us. Robert decided to take a bath and made Princess get in with him. While they were in the tub, he fondled her and stuck his tongue in her mouth. He threatened her by saying if she told me, I would never believe her. He told her he was sure I would beat her even harder for lying if she told me. Thus, Princess said nothing to either Coco or me.

As the weeks went by, Robert gave me less and less money to help with the household bills and food. He made good money, and I couldn't figure out why he seemed to have so little to contribute. In November when I relapsed, Robert didn't try to stop me. In fact, he smoked crack cocaine with me. He had been drugging all along. Finally I threw him out because he gave me no money to help with the bills. He stole my checks on his way out and tried to forge my name as he passed those bad checks in Florida.

After he was gone, Princess told Coco and me that she had a secret. As we coaxed her into the telling of her secret, we learned that Robert had fondled her. She had been afraid to tell us until Robert was long gone. Here's the sad note on my relationship with Robert: My cousin knew Robert was a pedophile. He had been convicted in the last city in which he had lived. Johnny and Frankie knew their friend did crack cocaine and kids but never said a word about it to me until he was gone.

Paul was my next man. I knew Paul from long ago, and we had always been friends. He started out as a roommate, but we eventually became lovers. Paul was an alcoholic but was kind and gentle. He tried to tell me crack cocaine was bad for me, but in the end, Paul did it with me. He did not like how others treated me. Folks would want to come and use my house to do their drugs but would not share with me. Paul would buy me my own drugs whenever he got paid.

When Paul first moved in, he slept on the sofa. I needed money, so Coco thought he was okay because he was helping us meet our bills. Paul always treated the kids and me well. He was a provider; he'd give the kids money for things they wanted like candy for Princess and cigarettes for Coco. Even after we became a couple, Paul still provided for us. He did his part as he helped me cook and clean. Paul was a good friend.

Paul had gone to prison before he moved in with us. He had taken the rap for his nephew. Being the kind-and-gentle soul he was, he would not snitch on his own family. He was charged with criminal trespassing and second-degree burglary and was put on probation since he had no previous record. He simply was trying to save his nephew's neck. While we were living together, the system caught up to him. He had not complied with his probationary rules. They arrested him and sent him to jail for four years. Paul continued to provide for us even while he was in prison sending me $200 a month to help keep my phone on so we could talk. I went down to see him in prison several times. When he got out, he was unable to find me because I was living with my brother Capt'n.

We eventually met up again, but nothing ever came of our reunion. The other bigger reason we didn't connect was I was clean, and he was not. At this point in my life, I had finally made the decision to never go back to the partying lifestyle. I had lost too much. Paul could not give up the drug that he had always told me was so bad.

After Paul, there was Simon. I had had so many bad boyfriends in my life; one would think I would learn. I met Simon on the bus coming home from Zoey's house. I was drunk, minding my own business, and ended up asking this man to my house.

Princess was in foster care, and Coco was dead; I was so alone. Looking back, I can't believe I was so low on myself to ever hook up with this kind of man. He came and asked to stay for just a few nights. His few nights turned into a few months' stay. We drank and smoked together, but Simon couldn't control his liquor.

Simon was filthy dirty, controlling, and loud. He is the only person I have ever met who went into the bathroom to clean up and came out just as smelly as he went in.

He never used soap or toothpaste. This was the only man who ejaculated on my couch and didn't clean up after himself.

Simon was both physically and verbally abusive. He was mean and demeaning to me, calling me fat and ugly. He'd slap me around unless his younger brother was around. He was afraid of Little Simon. The brothers were from Delaware and had, at one time, had a good life, owning lots of nice things. But I couldn't get rid of this son of a bitch.

I went to the Jefferson County jail at this time. My neighbor said I was playing my music too loud and had threatened him with a knife. I was thrown in jail for ten days since my dear sweet Simon wouldn't ante up $50 for my bail.

I took some of Simon's money one day to go to the store to buy a beer. We were always taking each other's money to buy liquor. That crazy man woke up and found me gone with some of his money. He came after me. When he found me, he took the beer I had bought and tried to hit me full force with that beer bottle. If I had not ducked in time, the sheer force of that bottle on my head probably would have killed me. I moved just in the nick of time.

Simon was eventually arrested for "failure to appear." I finally got rid of him when he went to jail. He had said that I owed him $25. I paid him in full while he was in jail and called it good and over!

Stuart and I were clean and sober together. We lived in the same apartment building, and we would drink coffee together every morning. Stuart was always gentle with me, and we were no more than sex buddies. He never wanted any commitments.

We could talk for hours, and I treasured his friendship.

Stuart was diagnosed with hepatitis. His new medication made him become far and distant. I lost my friend; he shut me out. Since I had lost my close friendship with Stuart, I began to pay attention to another guy, Jigalo, who was staying with his brother in our building. Before Stuart shut me out of his life, he had always warned me to stay clear of Jigalo as he was a loser. He said Jigalo was no good and a snake in the grass.

Stuart eventually married. He married a woman whom he met on the Internet. I was always good enough to be somebody's good time but never good enough to be his wife.

I began to hang out with Jigalo because he gave me the attention that I was missing from Stuart. Our relationship developed into a long-distance love affair because he went to prison for violating his parole. While in prison, Jigalo would call me and write me the most wonderful love letters. I would drive all the way to Limon and Burlington to visit him in prison. I supported him financially in prison for two years. I'd send money so he could have whatever he needed in prison. In the end, this man actually told me he was not attracted to me at all; he just wanted my money! You'd think I'd learn! Finally, Jigalo gave me a choice: either send him money and have him or use the money I had saved to buy my condo. Guess who finally got smart! I bought my condo. I was a homeowner!

I had a long-distance relationship with a guy named Justin. I met him once, made him wear a condom, and that was the last I ever saw of him. Justin was a truck driver. He would call me on the road, telling me he was cold and hungry and in need of money. I actually wired this dude money twice. This crazy relationship went on for a year. He was using all his money to buy crack cocaine. Imagine, all this for being with a guy only once!

The men in my life have brought me heartache, pain, abuse, and rarely love. I have become more cautious with time. My father tells me that my standards are too high, and I will never find a man who doesn't drink or do drugs. He tells me I am going to be an old maid. I have decided maybe being old and an old maid might be better than lowering my standards. I am still awaiting my dream man, and, Dad, my standards are NOT TOO HIGH!

COCO

Dear God,

    Please help me to get through and keep my mind focused on the memory of your gift to me: Coco DePaul Macey, born September 10,1978, in Denver, Colorado. He weighed six pounds eight ounces. He died November 16, 1996.

Love,
Rara

Coco was my passage to adulthood. My hopes and dreams were to be a better mother to my son than Sweets was to me. We were going to do a lot of great things like play and grow together and, most importantly, never leave one another. This is what I planned for Coco and me when he arrived on September 10, 1978. I desired a secure future for Coco and myself. I wanted us to be safe. I hoped Coco would have good self-esteem, be educated, and be very smart, and he would not be a criminal. I hoped I would be nurturing as a parent and love him with all my heart. I planned on being involved in his schooling. I wanted to take him to the zoo and be able to hang out with my baby. I was going to have a job and not be on welfare all my life. I had no desire to be an AFDC (Aid to Families with Dependent Children) recipient forever. Life with my baby, Coco, was going to be different than what I had had as a child. Coco would grow up to be the best at whatever sport he chose.

Coco, who had the skin the color of chocolate, was short and chunky with big, brown eyes. His eyes would make people want to smile at him. His laugh was so contagious that those around him laughed as well. He was a very happy and curious baby who liked being outside. Although at the beginning, he did not like walking a lot, nor did he like being in a stroller. He was always looking at insects, leaves, or flowers. He loved to put things in his mouth like dirt and rocks. While he was still in diapers, he could make a big stink! That baby could smell up an entire room, and thus we often called him "Stinker-Binker!"

I had my own place on 2110 Williams Street when Coco was born. I had saved for my Section 8 Housing so I could be alone with my baby. We were now our own family. However, as I described before, Sweets had come into my place while I was in the hospital and stole all my rent money for gambling and booze. After surviving for only six to seven months on my own, Coco and I were evicted. We were forced to return to Nanny's house.

Sweets was my main babysitter when I brought my baby home. Coco loved his granny. Sweets was delighted with her first grandson. It was as if my baby was continually wrapped in a Saran wrap of protection by Sweets. She loved to buy Coco clothes and toys. Looking back, I wonder if Sweets's attention to Coco was something she did out of guilt. She had been a lousy mother to me, and maybe she wanted to make up for it by being a good grandmother to my baby. With Sweets playing the role of mother to Coco, I was freed up to party and drink all I wanted. I was nineteen years old with a kid. Alcohol and the partying lifestyle took over. I was having fun! With my chosen partying path, I didn't know how to make all my dreams and hopes for Coco happen. I forgot those grand ideas for our future. I had a mother who was enabling my lifestyle and a mother who had never been a much parenting role model.

When we moved into Nanny's home, Sweets became less of a grandmother figure to my baby. If we were all out doing our thing, Nanny would care for the little ones.

Cece had a little boy, Morris, who was a year and a half older than Coco. My Coco was fascinated with his cousin and couldn't get enough playtime with that little boy. For the most part, everyone living at Nanny's house including Sweets, Andre, Cece, and myself were raising the children. Because Coco was such a sweet boy and Sweets's first grandchild, I believe that other various family members were jealous of little Coco from the beginning. He grabbed too much attention from everyone else. Cece never did love my baby because he took some of the attention away from her Morris.

One summer's day when Coco was about two years old, everyone was drinking and smoking pot. I wasn't in my right mind, and I think I wanted to impress those with whom I was hanging out. The game started with me swinging my baby round and round in circles; I was just playing with him. As that game became less fun, I upped the ante. I started to play catch with Coco as my ball. On a dare, I threw him, my ball, out a second story window of Nanny's house to my best friend. He caught him. My brother Andre chewed me out for doing that stunt. My family thought I was crazy and a terrible mother. The alcohol that I drank caused me to do crazy things. I needed help but had no one to turn to. If I told anyone who could help me, I knew they would take my baby away from me. I couldn't lose my Coco. I am not proud of what I did to Coco, but I did indeed do these things to my son. This was the beginning of many bad things that would happen to Coco.

Nanny took care of Coco and Morris much of the time while I tried to work or was out partying. Nanny didn't mind caring for the boys because when the adults were out of the house, she found some peace and quiet. These little boys were close and were the only small ones around Nanny's at this time. One day, I needed to run down to the corner store to get a money order for my next apartment's rent. I thought I was finally going to get out into my own place. Coco and I would have a new start. Cece was home with Morris, and she offered to watch Coco for me while I ran my errand. I should have never agreed to leave Coco in her care; Cece was mean to Coco.

Once I got my money order, I strayed to the corner liquor store for a drink. By the time I got back, Cece was screaming that something was wrong with Coco. My baby was running around in circles like a crazy child. Cece had decided to give the boys a bath. Coco was left in the tub of running hot water. He was burned on both his feet and hands. The water was so hot that it caused the removal of most of the skin in those areas. An ambulance rushed him to St. Joseph's Hospital. It killed me to see my baby's little feet and hands all wrapped up in bandages. They had his little hands elevated above his bed to help them heal. His hospital stay lasted two weeks. The part I could not understand was that there was not a scar on Morris, and they were both supposedly in the bathwater together. I wanted to file charges against Cece for harming my baby, but nobody would listen to my story. Cece was never blamed for my son's second- and third-degree burns. It took a year or so before I could get Coco into a tub of water.

Around the time, Coco was three years old. We were staying in Nanny's basement. Coco's daddy, Charles, asked Coco to come to bed with us. He actually told me that he would give me money if I would perform oral sex on Coco. He, too, wanted to play with and suck on Coco's little penis. When he began to touch Coco, he got really scared and crawled out of that bed. I couldn't believe this crazy man would do this to my son.

Charles was one bad, messed-up man. I began to realize that I was not able to protect my son from all the craziness surrounding me.

In our home at age four, Coco had a great Christmas. His Uncle Capt'n got him a big wheel tricycle and a bright-yellow Tonka truck. These two were his favorite toys. The kid would play outside for hours, riding his big wheel and playing with his truck. Coco had five uncles, and all of them were very fond of him. They mostly spoiled him with clothes, shoes, and toys. To be honest, they stuck around to watch him, in fear that I would get drunk and not care for my son. Sweets and her man, Don, were living with us at the time. My brother Capt'n came around every day to check on Sweets; her health was not good. Capt'n took great interest in Coco's upbringing. My brother Ernest took care of Coco a great deal of the time. He was a proclaimed Christian and involved in his church. He wasn't a drinker, but he provided alcohol for the rest of us. Coco was taught from a very early age to love Jesus by Ernest. His love of Jesus carried my Coco through many a hard time. I think at the time I didn't mind my brothers' interest, love, and support of Coco. I realized that I was not always in the best mind-set to care for my son.

We moved for the last time from Nanny's house in 1982. Coco and I had our own place in 1983. Before long, however, Sweets came to live with us. She supposedly was waiting for her own place to open up. Her temporary stay lasted for two long years. Next came Andre, and finally Sweets's boyfriend, Don, moved in as well. It seemed like every time I managed to finally get a place of my own, my mother and brother wiggled their way into my house. Sweets said she would help me care for Coco. During this time, my alcoholism increased as did my hanging out on 22nd Avenue.

The 22nd Avenue was a place to hang out. There was a big wall that everyone just sat on to pass the time away drinking from brown paper bags. There was a liquor store, a laundromat, and a gambling shack. I was having the time of my life! I learned how to panhandle on 22nd Avenue and earned the nickname "50qt" because all I ever asked for was 50 quarters. I was drunk all the time.

Living in the Twentieth Street house was one bad scene. It was about this time too when everybody flocked to my crib to drink and party. Coco was exposed to the worst that life has to offer. He experienced everything from alcohol, drug use, card playing, gambling, shooting dice to my brother Andre bringing his tricks to the house only to beat them out of their money. Everybody was doing their own thing. Sweets did the cooking for all of us, but she attracted gamblers to the house. Don was a quiet man, an alcoholic. He became Coco's grandpa and would take care of him if none of the rest of us were up to the task. I was drinking daily. I don't ever recall being sober during this time on 20th Street. It had become a way of life for all in my family.

Coco became my personal four-year-old water boy. I would get so sick from drinking that he would be the one to bring me water, something cold for my hangover. Coco would sometimes say, "Mama, pray and stop drinking the booze." My son never gave up on me. I guess this kid could sense what would happen next. If I kept on drinking, there was no way I could take care of him. My house was not a good environment for my little boy.

At four, Coco was able to attend Head Start. He loved school; it was a safe haven for him. In 1984, Coco was taken to the Crisis Center because he was left at the day-care center. No one came to pick him up. I was drunk and passed out at home. My brother Ernest was supposed to pick him up and never showed up. Once Coco was taken away, the authorities uncovered other abuses that had happened to my son. They even discovered that Ernest had fondled Coco. That Christian man had abused my son, but he never was prosecuted for that violation. He left town when he found out the authorities were onto him. I discovered this abuse only years later when Coco and I were in family therapy together. To protect my little boy, he was placed in foster care. He was gone for eight months.

Coco was placed in the wonderful care of Mrs. Luella Taylor. She was a kind Christian woman who loved my son as her own. Luella was laid-back and demonstrated love for everybody she met. She cared for my baby and gave him security and normalcy.

Coco returned home and life was back to normal. The only difference was that we moved to another house on Lafayette Street. I wanted a fresh start for us. I even bought Coco a TV in an effort to make new beginnings. I was determined to do things right. Again, here came my mother, her boyfriend, and my brother Andre. As before, my family took over my home, and I lost all control. This round, Andre took the TV that I bought Coco. He sold it so he could have money to buy drugs.

Coco lasted at home only four months before he was placed once again in foster care. A neighbor called Social Services because they saw Coco running around the street dirty and uncared for. He was not attending school. I lost Coco a second time, and he was gone for eleven years. The only relief from having Coco gone was that he wound up in Luella Taylor's care.

Mother Taylor never gave up on Coco or me. She often told me that she loved him as her own son. She continued to pray for me because this boy needed his own mother. Luella was a religious woman as was her family. Her brother was a preacher, and her sister provided food and care to the homeless. Coco was often involved in the ministries in which Luella's family participated. I believe that during the time he spent with Mother Taylor, Coco was exposed to God in many good ways, including prayer, attending church, and doing for others. If I had not been so afraid of life without alcohol and drugs, I might have opened myself up more genuinely to Mother Taylor. She knew how to parent. And looking back, I feel sure she could have and would have taught me so much about how to be a mother. Life for Coco and me might have turned out so differently with Luella Taylor's mentoring.

Mother Taylor did a great job of raising Coco those eleven years. She was his way out to a better world, and she provided him with a stable, loving environment. Chances were a million to one that he landed with her the second time in foster care, but he did. She loved and cared for him as her own child. Her only son was past forty years old. Coco never complained about Mrs. Taylor. He would always say good things concerning her. She kept him inspired and encouraged. She taught him to be respectful of his elders. Luella told him that he was a good, smart boy with lots of talent. She nurtured him as a mother should.

I was overwhelmed with sadness and anger. My Lafayette house was supposed to have been for Coco and me only. But my damn family had to come in. I didn't have the courage to tell them no. I didn't know how to function without my dysfunctional, crazy family. I was so frustrated that I broke every window out of my house. I wanted those damn people out of my house! I wanted to get my baby back. It was too late; Coco was.

During the eleven years that Coco was in foster care, he was allowed to come to my house for weekend visits. I would have a review every six months. However, I would be drunk and not show up to my court dates or keep my appointments with Coco. I let my son down over and over again.

In 1987 when Princess was born, Coco was my little helper on the weekends that he came to be with us. I was smoking crack cocaine by this time, and when I was too busy doing my drugs, he would watch his sister. Coco became very attached to Princess and wanted to always protect her.

One night, Tommy tried to jump me and beat me up while I was holding Princess in my arms. I called the police to protect myself from this crazy man. When the police came, they wanted to take Princess out of our violent home and were willing to release her only to her grandmother. When I called Sweets to ask her to come and take Princess, she replied that she was too busy gambling right then, but she would send Capt'n over to get her. My mother was gambling, too busy! When Capt'n came for Princess, the police would not give her to him. She was taken away to a foster home. I lost my baby girl. I blamed my mother for my loss, not myself. Drugs and alcohol were my priorities. When I went to the family court where Princess's fate would be decided, I requested that Princess remain in foster care until I could get myself together. This was difficult decision for me to make, but I needed help!

Mother Taylor was also crazy about Princess, whom she called "Peaches," and she arranged for my two kids to visit each other often. My children remained close thanks to Luella Taylor. It was a strange relationship for Coco to be in one foster home and Princess in another. He loved his sister, and he had taken care of her. My kids had bonded, and they managed to stay close, thanks to Mother Taylor.

Shortly after relinquishing my children to the system, I went to prison. My desires to get sober and clean didn't materialize. I met failure after failure. I tried Antabuse, alcoholic classes, parenting classes, and outpatient treatment. My caseworkers didn't give up on me. They saw something in me that allowed them to believe in me. They didn't take away my ADFC support even though my kids were not with me. They worked with me to get me in the right places for help. I needed help; I asked for help.

My innermost self was crying for help. So what happened? Fear? I was afraid. I never knew life without alcohol and drugs. My family members never functioned sober. I didn't know how to live a clean and sober life. I had no friends or acquaintances who were not alcoholics or druggies.

My house became a flophouse. People came to my house to smoke crack cocaine and to buy drugs. I had become a drug dealer.

There were tweakers coming and going. Tweakers are drug users who bring new drug customers to your door. They are continually knocking on the door; they show up every five to ten minutes. Tweakers are also snitches who threaten to turn you into the police unless you provide them with some free drugs. This dude would give me the drugs, and then I used my house to sell them. I was not a big fish to be caught, but I was dealing drugs. When the transportation came to my house to pick up my kids from a visiting weekend, I was very jittery. I lied about being high on crack cocaine. I told her I had smoked a joint that had been laced with crack cocaine. That admission meant that I lost the chance to win my kids back for another six months and brought suspicion to my house.

The police searched my house after this encounter. They were hoping that by raiding my house, they might find the big drug dealers. They found a gun, residue from crack cocaine, and forty Valium pills for which I had no prescription. They never caught the main dealer, but I was arrested and sentenced to two years in prison. I served five months before going onto a halfway house.

Once I was released from the halfway house, I was placed on parole for one year with the conditions of going to support groups, remaining drug free, and getting a job.

The interesting thing about this time of my life was that my parole officer had also been my father's parole officer. He took a special interest in me and encouraged me to get my life straightened out. However, I came up with a dirty UA (urine analysis) and had thus violated my parole. My parole officer took a chance on me and gave me one of two choices: I could go back to prison for one year or commit myself to an intensive inpatient twenty-one-day treatment program. I took the program, got myself clean and off parole.

I found myself at Empowerment seeking help and services from the very folks I would eventually work for. I was able to reconnect with my kids and have visitations with them. However, my renewal was short-lived. I returned to my crack-cocaine usage and lost my way again. This time, the system threw me out. I lost my Section 8 Housing and my ADFC funding. There were no more chances; the plug was finally pulled. I was higher than a kite the day I was evicted and decided I'd fix "them." I rented a moving truck and removed all the appliances out of the home. The washer/dryer combo, the stove, and the refrigerator all went into the truck sitting outside the evicted house in broad daylight. I was going to sell everything and have plenty of money for my next round of drugs. I'd show them! However, the neighbors called the police, and I was arrested for criminal trespassing and harboring stolen property. Because of my criminal record that was forever following me, I could have been given four to six years in prison. But, again, good luck came my way. I think good people just never gave up on me. I was given the choice of prison or enter into the Cenikor program. I chose Cenikor.

I spent 1992–1994 in Cenikor. I was finally clean and sober for two and a half years. Cenikor helped me get clean, but I was never rehabilitated. I was not taught how to survive without alcohol and drugs in the real world. I didn't know how to meet people who were not drinking and drugging. I knew how to work, pay my bills, keep my house, but I didn't know how not to be lonely. Cenikor was a closed environment; I was protected from the outside, but when I came out, I had learned no skills to survive without drugs and alcohol.

While in Cenikor, Coco and I did therapy together. I learned how angry he was at me, at Ernest for molesting him, at the world. It was recommended that he do individual therapy sessions, but he refused. He was still living with Mrs. Taylor. He was picked up for shoplifting at Walmart but was not prosecuted. He had learned how to smoke cigarettes and pot at Zoey's house. Luella had diabetes, and one day she found Coco smoking in her house. The smoke aggravated her disease, and she asked Coco to leave. I think it probably killed her to ask him to leave because she had given him so much and cared for him as her own. Luella Taylor was true to Coco in that she meant what she said, and he did not respect and honor her rules. She stood by her word. If only he could have hung on a little longer. He moved in with Capt'n, and things went downhill. Capt'n was like a drill sergeant with Coco. Capt'n found Coco smoking pot at Zoey's house and got very angry with Coco, grounding him for the entire summer. He was not allowed to go outside the house. Coco was more than angry, and Capt'n quit bringing my kids to see me at Cenikor.

Coco told me to hurry it up because if I didn't come home soon to get him, he was going to hurt his crazy uncle. I begged Coco to hang on and told him that we would soon be together. Coco believed me, but the damage was done.

Two and a half years later, I won my kids back! We were off to a fresh start. In March of 1995, we all moved together, Coco, Princess, and me to Lakewood, Colorado. Coco was a handsome young man. He was also a very smart kid who carried a GPA of 4.0 at George Washington High School. He had dreams of going to MIT or Colorado School of Mines because he wanted to be an engineer or work with computers. He had such wonderful dreams. However, I relapsed in November of 1995. I was afraid of the people in my new world. My family was all I knew. I had changed; they had remained the same. I had not learned how to live life on life's terms. I had not found a way to live this new nonalcoholic, drug-free life. It hurt him deeply when I relapsed in November 1995. Coco loved his mother; he just couldn't help me quit drugs and booze.

It was Thanksgiving of 1995. I had been clean and sober for two and a half years when Ernest and I planned a big Thanksgiving dinner for our family at my house. I wish I could have been stronger. As the family began to arrive, I was upstairs getting dressed, and I drank a beer to calm my nerves. Coco came in to check on me and saw me drinking my beer. I'll never forget; he said, "Dude, what are you doing?" I yelled at him to get out of my face because I was going to drink that beer. I don't know why I didn't listen to my son. I was scared to greet my family on my own terms. I was eleven months out of Cenikor before this relapse.

Each relapse was always worse than the last one. I washed two and a half years of hard work down the toilet with that beer. That Thanksgiving, I went back to my old ways. I was more calculating with my drinking and drugging this time. I actually applied for unemployment before I even quit my job the following April. I made sure I had bought all of the things Coco needed for his graduation such as his senior pictures, his cap and gown, and the other incidentals that accompany graduation. My baby was going to graduate no matter what. I quit my job so I could drink and do my crack cocaine.

By the time Coco graduated in May of 1996, I was smoking crack cocaine full time.

I was so proud of my son graduating. But not proud enough to show up to his graduation sober. I reeked of alcohol when Princess and I went to the convention center to watch him to receive his diploma. I felt bad about my alcoholic state. But I tried. I threw my newly graduated son a party, but he never showed up. Coco knew there would be plenty of alcohol and drugs at his party. He knew his family would show up to his celebration mainly for the booze and drugs that he knew would be present. He wanted no part of it. I didn't blame him. I was a huge failure. I had let my boy down yet again.

Coco was an introvert. I didn't always know what was on his mind. He told me over and over again that he was a leader and not a follower. He did life on his terms. He took good care of himself and his little sister. He was always so protective of Princess. He did his best to save me. I remember Coco begging me during this time to please smoke pot instead of crack cocaine. The problem was I could not get a high off of pot. My addictions had returned with a vengeance.

My drinking and smoking went out of control. Coco and Princess had to fend for themselves. My neighbors called Social Services on Princess's behalf. They reported that she was running amuck on the streets dirty, unkempt, and unfed. I lost Princess again but not Coco as he was old enough to take care of himself. He pleaded with me to get my act together so I could get Princess back. He was afraid she would be lost to the system the way he had been for eleven years.

During this time, Coco was working at university hospital doing data entry. He gave me the money he earned to help pay the bills. I believe he probably knew I used much of that money to continue to buy booze and crack cocaine, but he never said anything. My baby helped support my habit while he continually asked me to stop and get help. The month before he died, I promised I would seek that help.

I did indeed manage to get clean again in August for one month. However, my poor choice of acquaintances and friends ended by being attacked on Labor Day, 1996. I was left for dead. When I returned home, the pain, the sorrow, the guilt, everything was too much for me to face. Relapse set in again. My relapse was Coco's last. My son had to die in order for me to be saved. I think we learn so much about our loved ones through death. Coco died November 16, 1996.

It was a Friday night, and Coco had just been paid. Coco got stinking drunk. It was the only time I ever saw my boy drunk. He came home late and was so drunk he couldn't fit his key into the front door. I got up to let him in. I was high myself, so I didn't say anything to him. Besides, what could I say to my son about drinking? The next day, we were sitting around, just hanging out together, and he offered me some of his Cinnabons. Coco loved those sweet rolls! He also gave me a Miller Genuine Draft. I took it but told him I was going to save it because I was heading down to visit Paul in prison the next day. I didn't drink when I went to see Paul. I was cold sober that day, all day.

I went up to bed around ten in the evening. Coco was in the basement with his two pals, Jesus and Ralph; the boys were the best of friends. Both Jesus and Ralph were Hispanic kids; Jesus was a handsome kid, and Ralph was younger than the other two boys. Both Jesus and Ralph were gang members; Coco was never in the gang; he just had gang affiliations. Jesus and Coco were pedaling crack. Neither boy used because they both had first-hand experience with how it destroyed people's lives. Jesus's mother would smoke crack cocaine with me. I even stole some crack rocks from the boys. Coco never accused me of the theft, but Jesus stole sixty of my CDs to pay himself back for what I had taken.

Early Sunday morning around three, I heard a knock on the front door. I woke up from a deep sleep and stumbled down the stairs thinking it was Coco again, unable to get his key in the door. I was stunned to find the police at my door. They told me to stay put as they had received a call from a young lady who claimed she had heard a gun go off while she was talking to Coco. When the police went downstairs, they found Coco dead from a gunshot to the head. He had shot himself in the temple. I did not go down to see my son but was able to identify him by saying that if he had on khaki pants, a khaki shirt over a black T-shirt with black combat boots, then it was my boy, Coco. My baby was dead.

I returned upstairs, shocked, overwhelmed, and distraught. The police cleaned up the basement, and I didn't go down there for a long time. I did go visit Paul the next day as planned; I didn't know what else to do. Jesus and Ralph were questioned, but neither was ever under in suspicion for foul play. However, that Saturday night in the wee morning hours as the police came through my living room, a red handkerchief was spread out on my living room floor in front of the coffee table. It was a sign from the gang honoring Coco.

I don't remember much about planning Coco's funeral. I only recall picking out the suit he was to be buried in and that I wore the peach-colored suit he had help me pick out and bought for me to his funeral. His wake was at Zoey's house since the family saw my house as too far for everyone to come to pay their last respects. I was in a state of shock and could not make decisions about anything. I never saw a dime of any donations that were made in Coco's name. Not one dime. My family took care of all of those details too.

As we went to the funeral, Princess, Londel, his girlfriend, Sandy, Caspar, and myself were the only ones in the family car. I would not allow Cece to ride with us. Mother Taylor chose to drive her own car. It was an open casket, and you could not tell Coco had shot himself in the head. I did not go up to view his body; I was too drunk and too numb. There was standing room only, and a few of his friends spoke of him. They recounted how Coco was warm, caring, loving, and had a smile that was so bright it would light up any room. My Cenikor family was present; they had not given up on me and were there to love and support me.

Coco was buried at Riverside Cemetery. As people walked by his casket, a red cloth was dropped into the grave with my baby. I was able to buy a headstone for my son's grave but not until 2000. It took me that long to do something for my son. I bought that headstone all by myself to ask him his forgiveness for a lifetime of sorrow.

From the Sunday that Coco died to the following Friday of his burial, I tried everything I could do to get high. Nothing worked no matter how hard I tried. The hurt was so profound that nothing would make it go away. I contemplated suicide as I looked down the stairs to Coco's room but couldn't do it because of Princess. Coco wanted me to get her back, and I knew I had to do that for him and for her.

I stayed in the Lakewood house until the following April. I cleaned out Coco's things. I gave everything away. I didn't want anything to remind me of my lost son. As time has gone by, I wish I had saved so many of the things I gave away for myself and for Princess. I only have the memories in my heart of my dearest boy.

I know that Coco was liked by everyone because he had a very large funeral. I know that my son is my heavenly angel. I know, without a doubt, that his prayers were finally answered when I got clean in 1998. Overall, my son was a great kid. He was smart, fine, and very respectable. He was a healthy child with a lot of love for his sick mother. As far as I know, he wasn't really into sports. He told me he was a leader, not a follower. Every one of my cousins tried to get him to be a bad boy. But my boy finished school; he was not involved in gangs and had no juvenile record. Yes, he did smoke pot and probably was popular with the young girls, but he used condoms and was loyal to his steady girlfriend. I only saw him drink one time, and that was the night before he took his own life. During the years on Twentieth Avenue, Coco saw a lot of bad things including beatings, drug and alcohol use and abuse, stealing as well as being neglected by his own mother. But my Coco chose to live a good life instead of succumbing to the poisons that has ruined so many of those whom he loved. My angel in heaven will hopefully forgive his mother for all her weaknesses. I have asked for his forgiveness over and over. There are no do-overs in this life.

PRINCESS

Princess is my reason for being. She is the reason I have found a will to live. She is the most important person in my life. This was not always the case.

Princess was born February 2, 1987. How I got pregnant with her after being able to avoid pregnancy for eight years, I do not know. Looking back, I think I probably failed to show up to get my birth-control shot which generally kept me safe for ninety days. Tommy was Princess's father, and as I have already described, he was a mean and violent man. He already had two daughters; Princess would make his third. He really didn't have much concern about my being pregnant. He never asked me how I was feeling or how my doctor's appointments went. There was really no talk between us about the baby we were going to have. Tommy would say now and again that we were going to be a family but little else. I was afraid of Tommy, and he controlled me; rather than say too much, I just kept the peace.

I can remember being excited about having a brand-new baby in the house. Once again, I thought it might be my ticket to get myself together. When my new baby arrived, I would get myself clean and sober. However, in the meantime, I continued to drink, smoke cigarettes, and did some crack cocaine. Princess was born four weeks early and was very small. She weighed all of three pounds four ounces. I never really experienced any kind of contractions with her. My water just broke, and I had no labor; I had been on a crack-cocaine bender when she came. Tommy was on the road, so my cousin called the ambulance, and away I went to the hospital. My baby girl's birth was as uneventful as my pregnancy with her.

My Princess was a beautiful, tiny, very dark baby girl. For one being so tiny, she had one huge head of black shiny hair. Her hands were so little, and she had big ol' eyes. I remember being delighted as she would wiggle and wiggle her tiny body when I changed her. Princess was jaundiced when I brought her home. The doctor told me she needed sunlight to help her get better. I can remember a bright, sunny day in February, and I had her propped up on a pallet that my brother Ernest had arranged for her so she could absorb the sunlight streaming through the oval living-room window. My house was a shotgun house, which meant when you opened up the front door, you could see straight to the back of the house. I was on my way into the bathroom at the back of the house when I saw Princess tumble forward off the pallet onto the floor. I was so scared for my baby girl. She was fine, but what a vivid memory I have of her falling that day.

Ernest was around lots when Princess arrived. He was thrilled with his new niece and often helped me care for her. Ernest was also an enabler in that he would buy me booze, although he made sure we had plenty of food in the house as well. Ernest and Tommy were good friends, and in the end, crack cocaine ended up overpowering Ernest.

Sweets was taken with Princess too. She loved this tiny baby girl. However, since I had outgrown my partying and bar days, Sweets did not care for Princess as much as she had for Coco. Sweets let me down big time one night when Princess was two months old. Tommy had come home and was threatening Princess and me. I called the police on him; I was afraid he might hurt our little girl. When the police showed up at the door, they wanted to remove Princess from our violent home. The only person they would release her to in the family was my mother. When I called Sweets asking her to come and get my baby, she sent Capt'n instead as she was all tied up in a gambling game. Since Capt'n was not the grandmother, they would not give her to him. The police took Princess to the Crisis Center, and from there, she was placed in a foster home. I had lost my little girl only after two months.

The lifestyle in a crack house, my house, was not good. I was dealing drugs at this time, so people were constantly coming and going at all hours of the day and night. When alcohol came on the scene, things would get out of hand with people fighting or just being loud and obnoxious. It was not a peaceful environment for babies or anyone else for that matter. I wasn't ready to give up my drinking and drugging, but I was done with these loud, crazy people. I had wanted to be a mommy, but I wanted to drink too, just without all the damn people in my house. I didn't know how to make a new start because all my life, I had allowed people to walk all over me and take advantage of me. There was so much guilt in my heart about the use of alcohol and drugs. Princess had not had a fair start from the beginning because of my alcohol, drug, and cigarette usage. My nutrition during my pregnancy was poor; I did manage to take my prenatal vitamins, but I did little else to care for the little girl growing in my womb. She was born a fetal alcohol baby and would be diagnosed with ADHD. Princess has also demonstrated behavioral problems throughout much of her life. To top it off, I had lost her to Social Services after only two months. There had been too much chaos from the beginning with Princess.

When Princess was taken the first time, she was put in the care of a wonderful foster mother who dealt well with children with special needs. She was a nurse and loved Princess as her own. I called her a mini Mother Taylor. Both my children had landed in foster care with wonderful women. However, Princess's first foster-care situation lasted for about two years before the woman had to give up Princess to another home. Her own son was coming home from prison on parole, and she had to relinquish her day-care license so he could live with her in her home.

Unfortunately, Princess was bounced from home to home until she was four years old. I don't know for sure what all happened to my baby in these homes. But based on several behaviors I have experienced over the years with Princess, I do believe she encountered emotional, physical, and sexual abuse. Princess would do well with counseling, but she has not taken that step yet.

My brother Capt'n went through the Denver court system to gain guardianship of Princess. Capt'n was there from the beginning with Princess and wanted to take care of her. Since he was the only family member interested in taking care of Princess, the courts finally awarded him guardianship when Princess was four. I have to say Capt'n did a good job with my baby, although he was much too rigid and stern with her; he still is. He was also very protective of her.

Princess was a wild and wily little one, and I remember her having casts a few times on her arms or legs when Capt'n would bring her to see me. Princess was confused much her young life about who was the parent and boss in her life. When I got her back at age eight, she often would not listen to me as Uncle Capt'n had always been the one who was in charge of her. Where Coco always treated me as his mother, Princess saw me as a stranger. She would look at me, and I could tell she was thinking, "Who do you think you are telling me what to do when you haven't even been here!" I can't blame her, and it is still a challenge for her to accept me as her mother today.

There were times when I did not agree with what Capt'n did with Princess. I remember once when he brought her to see me at Cenikor. She had long hair extensions down to her waist. I thought it was far too old and sassy of a look for a little four-year-old girl. If Capt'n had to work, he would take Princess to Zoey's house. She did day care back in those days. Zoey's house was not the best place for her, but I had no say as I was not in the capacity to be her mother. Zoey's was where the family gatherings usually took place, and drugs and alcohol were almost always present. I worried and still do about the family's influence on Princess as they have never been a good influence on me.

Capt'n and Princess have a very tight bond; he was her safe haven. Capt'n treated her like his own daughter, for better and worse. Princess was not allowed to do much without restrictions. If she was out in the yard with her roller blades on, she was only allowed to go from point A to point B, all of about fifteen feet. She had to dress a certain way, sit in her room and read for x number of minutes, and make her bed. Princess was fearful of her uncle, although she rarely complained about him.

After my stay in Cenikor, I regained custody of both my children. Once Princess, Coco, and I moved to Lakewood for our new life together, I gave both my kids more freedom to play and be outside than they had ever had. Princess was a free little bird going all over the neighborhood to play because she had not had an opportunity to do before with Capt'n or in her foster homes.

When I relapsed after my Cenikor experience, I lost Princess to Social Services again. One of my neighbors turned me in for allowing Princess to run around the neighborhood unattended, dirty, and underfed. Due to my return to alcohol and drug usage, I was not caring for my little girl as I should have. Since we now lived in Jefferson County, Princess was placed in foster homes there. When Capt'n found out she was no longer living at home with Coco and me, he once again went through the court system to gain guardianship of Princess.

After Coco's death, I was lost in a sea of anger, mourning, and depression. I drank and drugged to avoid feeling all my losses and hopelessness. However, when I climbed out to that huge, dark, deep hole, I petitioned the courts to get my little girl back from my brother. I had to prove to them that I could remain sober and clean for one year. I chose to live with Capt'n and Princess for the next eleven months in an effort to claim my daughter for one last time. I paid my brother $200 a month and bought all my own food with my food stamps while living there. Capt'n was as rigid with me as he was with Princess.

During this long eleven months, I had to eat some huckleberry pie. I watched my brother parent Princess in a strict and often harsh manner, but I did not say too much as I wanted to win her back for good. Once while we were out shopping together, Princess stole a few Giga Pets from Walgreens; she loved those silly pretend pets. When Capt'n found out, he held her up off the ground with one hand while he spanked her with his shoe. Princess was often confused about who she should listen to when it came to anything and everything. I had been away, and Capt'n had been the father figure, but he was often too harsh. And she preferred my gentler ways. She played us against each other, as all kids will do; I generally gave in to Capt'n as he was stronger, and we were in his house.

As these long eleven months continued, I became more determined than ever to stay clean and sober so I could win my daughter back. I was learning how to be a good mother to my daughter and provide her with some of the things she really needed. I remember her eleventh birthday so well. Princess wanted to invite all her little cousins to a pizza party for her birthday. This would be the first birthday party I gave for my daughter all by myself. We rode the bus to Zoey's house to pick up the little folks, and then we continued on our way to Pizza Hut. We had lots of pizza and coke while Uncle Timmy brought Princess her own birthday cake. We took lots of pictures that day. It was a full-blown birthday party; I don't know who was happier, Princess or me!

My Princess was a strange little person in many ways. All her little life, she has had a complex about her very dark skin color and her hair. When it came time for me to fix her hair, she would have a fit. Her last foster mother had refused to comb her hair because she said she didn't know how to comb a black child's hair. Her hair became too matted and unruly to fix. To this day, she sometimes lacks self-confidence that is demonstrated in her inability to maintain her hygiene and personal appearance as she should. I tell her every chance I get how pretty she is, and when she makes an effort to fix her hair, brush her teeth, and put on clean clothes, I compliment her on her beauty.

Our relationship was complicated by Coco's death. Princess wanted to talk about him whenever we were together; she would say how much she missed him, how she wished we could go visit him, how she just wanted to be with her brother. I was not ready to talk about Coco with Princess or anyone for that matter for many years to come. I would have to finally say to her that we were not going to talk about Coco. She would honor that request until the next time she felt a need to bring him up.

I was able to get my daughter back when she was twelve years old, and I have not lost her again since. I have been there at all the major stepping stones in her life. When Princess got her first period,

I bought her some pads, a card, and teddy bear welcoming her into the world of womanhood. We made a vow together that she would not have anything to do with boys until she was sixteen, and that is exactly what happened. I was present at every ceremony in which she received an award from school; she made the principal's list as an honor student. I showed up clean and sober to celebrate her success. The day she graduated from East High School, I was there dressed to the nines, to honor and cheer my baby girl's high school graduation. I was so proud of her and me as we had both reached a milestone in our lives. Princess with her diploma and me being there clean and sober.

I treasure my daughter for all she is, and we continue on our life journey together even when the tough times come. Princess loves to be held and kissed. She asks me to kiss her first on her forehead, then each of her cheeks, to her nose, and finally on her lips. In all honesty, I still find it hard to embrace her at times today, as I don't know if my hug portrays all that I hold so dear. When I get ready to go out the door, she will just start saying, "Mama." When I ask her what she wants, rarely can she tell me. I wonder if she is afraid I will leave her again.

I have tried to provide for my Princess like I was never able to or capable of when Coco was alive. I think, in many ways, I am as much her mooring line in life as she is mine. Princess has never been without a space to call her own. She can be lazy, sloppy, unmotivated, but it doesn't matter. Princess will always have a place to call her own in my home. I will always be there for her no matter what comes our way. Because of my choice to do drugs and alcohol for so long, I missed out on more than any mother ever should. I know what I have to do to stay clean and sober, and I have learned to remain that way at all costs over the past ten years. I want a relationship with my daughter, and no matter what, I will always, always be there for Princess.

My Princess is smart, beautiful, and so capable of anything she sets her mind to do. Princess has a desire to serve elderly people. She can sit and listen to them for hours on end. Her life's goal today is to become a nurse so she can help care for the elderly. I see that as a true vocation and one not shared by many. She will be the best in caring for these people!

Princess has begun to spend time with her extended family and, like me, is beginning to experiment with pot usage at their houses. I am talking with her about what happens with drug and alcohol usage and how my family is not the best choice in friends. I am hoping with my genuine interest in her and my openness with our family history that Princess will become responsible in her behaviors and choices. I have made so many bad choices for so long that I would do anything to help my daughter walk down a different path. Princess is so much like me in her desire to be a part of a family. I just want us both to realize the reality that we may have to choose life over family.

SYSTEMS, BROKEN SYSTEMS

I have made many choices, good and bad, in my life, and I accept full responsibility for those choices. However, as I look back at my life's journey, many societal systems enabled me to choose the paths I chose. These systems are so ingrained in our American society that we don't often pay any attention to them, nor do we address the problems of those organizations in an effort to make them better or more accountable.

The first huge institution I encountered which has steered me wrong is the church. From the time I was a little girl, I can remember church people trying to make me something I am not. Nanny with her fire-and-brimstone lectures frightened me from the very beginning. She had condemned me to hell at the tender age of twelve, and I believed her! However, instead of steering me clear of alcohol, drugs, and the loose life I was about to choose, her ongoing threats of hell, me being the devil, me being a hopeless case only turned me away from my Creator and my Savior. I became her prophesy in many ways. Grandma Macey's introduction to the Bible only fed my fury against organized religion. There was no room for a girl like me in that book nor her harsh holy attempts to make me into whom she thought I should be. Over the years, I have belonged to numerous churches because I have wanted to belong to a home where I could worship God and serve Him to my fullest capacity. I am still searching for that church where I can be seen as a precious human being and be accepted by church members for who I am and not who they want me to be.

I can point to Jesus as the one who finally saved me from my tragic life's path. He reached out his hand in the ravine in which I was left to die, and I never let go. I took hold of His hand and chose

Him to be my Savior, and I have never looked back. I see myself as a deeply spiritual woman who tries to honor my God with all I am. I see my life as one of service to His people. However, when I have tried to join in any organized religion in an effort to share my faith, to grow in my faith, and to bring faith to my daughter, members of various congregations have judged me harshly for my life's choices. I am at peace with my relationship with my God, and I know I have made the worst of mistakes most of my life, but He has forgiven me and values me for who I am. Why do those who preach the gospel refuse to genuinely welcome me into their church family without passing judgment on me?

I think we are called to our various churches not only because of faith but also because of our ancestry. We worship in a particular church because our mamas did, our grandmother did, and our great-grandmother did. So many times, we find ourselves in a church/faith out of respect for our family traditions and not because we are in search of a relationship with God. We do things because that is how things have always been done. The tough questions are not asked or confronted out of respect to our elders, and we are therefore lost in our search for truth. If we were to live as Jesus demonstrated with his own life, we would not be excluding any one person for who he/she is or where he/she has been. We would be caring for our poor, homeless, less fortunate, and those on the margins without any pre-qualification. We would help each other with food, clothing, heating bills, housing instead of building huge megachurches which cost all of us too much to maintain and sustain.

Many of the folks who were in places of power at the various churches I have joined were my harshest judges. I would sing too loud for the choir director. I offended fellow church members with my testimony when describing the places I had been and the choices I had made. My life's path was not acceptable for a churchgoing member. I didn't add enough money in the offering plate. The truer I have tried to be in practicing and sharing my faith and relationship with God, the more I have been shunned by those in churches. In the end, my spirituality has been best nurtured by my own daily prayer, my own praise of my Maker, and my sharing of my own funds with those I see in my daily life who are in genuine need.

In many ways, my experience with church has been like joining a cult. I felt they have tried to brainwash me into following all their rules, contributing to all they say is important, and singing only as loud as they perceive as appropriate. So many times I have felt like the churches have preyed upon those most in need of God's love and mercy; those who have the least to give and the most to gain. As I have watched numerous fellow churchgoers drive up in their big fancy cars, dressed in their silk suits and mink coats, I wonder where did all my tithing money go? The more I was willing to give of myself, the more I was asked. If I didn't ante up, I was shunned. The church institutions in which I have belonged and participated have not proven to practice what they have preached. Churches are meant to bring souls in, not put them out the door. They ask "Where you been?" and not "How you been?" There is no human being who has a heaven or a hell to place me in. The church system in my life has been broken and has nearly broken me more than once.

Another system that has touched my life over and over again is the welfare or social-services systems. From the beginning, I have been a participant in welfare. Once my daddy chose the criminal path he did and Sweets became a welfare member, my life's path was chosen for many years as well. In the black community, welfare was a way of life. In the days before the Reagan and Clinton administrations, welfare supported women having babies and doing little else. The more children one had the bigger her check. There were few incentives to do something else with your life other than to lie on your backside and have babies. Sweets had a real job a couple of times where she was making a paycheck, but those jobs never lasted long. Why would she get up and go to work when she could collect more money through welfare? Monthly checks, food stamps, and subsidized housing were easier than figuring out day care, scheduling, decent job clothing, etc. As long as she had those babies dependent on her with no man in her life to help support her, the welfare checks just kept rolling in. The same became true for me by the age of nineteen. I stayed in the welfare system for many years, never dreaming of improving my life. It was so easy! If you don't have anything and everyone around doesn't have nothing, you don't know any different.

Life for me was like the lives of so many of the women I counsel today. We are all broken vessels with little or no self-esteem. There have not been people in our lives who have encouraged us or believed in us enough for us to dream beyond the welfare system. More is expected of welfare participants today than ever before. Women are required to go to school, work toward and receive their GED's if they have not graduated from high school. There is job training available as well as parenting classes and counseling sessions for women to attend. There is more encouragement for women to become self-sufficient and independent. Women must participate in betterment programs in order to continue to receive welfare help. Day care is provided for little folks while their mothers are attending various training classes. In the end, a woman has five years to reach a goal of self-sufficiency. If she fails, she is done. The system does not allow her to continue indefinitely without making progress toward living on her own.

The welfare system has indeed improved since I have become self-sufficient. However, for most of the years during which I benefited from welfare checks, food stamps, and Section 8 Housing, I played the system for all I could get. I was not motivated to better myself, nor did I have the self-esteem or the know-how to make it on my own. There was no accountability for me to do anything else. Even when I lost my children to Social Services, I continued to receive money and food stamps; my drugging and boozing were enabled by the system. I didn't have to make any other life choices; I could use the money to buy my addictive substances and still find ways to live and survive.

People may judge me harshly for using the system the way I did and not stepping up to the plate to care for my own children. Once again, I did what I knew; welfare had been a way of life for my family members. Drinking, drugging, and partying was my tradition, and I did not know how to live life without my traditions or family. I cannot remember a time other than my earliest years where this was not my reality. Developing friendships or relationships that did not include drugs and alcohol were not within my realm of being or even knowing how to survive that lifestyle. As for my children, I allowed others to care for them much as others had cared for me. As a mother, I knew I wanted to provide for Coco and Princess, but I didn't know how to do that. There were various people who came along my way who may have tried to teach me another way, but it was too foreign for me to embrace. Living without drugs, alcohol, and partying was a concept I just didn't get, and it was too frightening to try to do on my own. As long as nobody held me accountable for my behaviors and choices, I just kept going the only way I had really ever known.

The school system is another place where kids are often left to their own devices. Again, I am not saying my life choices were anyone's fault but my own, but I am a smart person. I wish school could have been more interesting to me than drinking at the corner bar. I wish I could have had parents who felt getting an education was the way to become self-sufficient and successful. I wish I could have had a magic teacher in my life who had taken me under his or her wing and encouraged me to dream bigger dreams and not settle for a life on welfare. I wish I could have had someone in the world that believed in me and thought I was capable of becoming something other than a welfare recipient. To do well in school, one has to have lots of folks who believe kids are capable of learning and becoming who they want to become. As a broken vessel that had been physically, emotionally, and sexually abused from a very early age, I needed an anchor somewhere in my life. The only anchors I found were the old men who would pay me some attention and buy me booze. That way of life was at least interesting, and I thought someone cared about me. Of course, now I know they didn't care about me at all; they were after only one thing, and it was not my wonderful mind! I have discovered that I love to learn, and I am a good student. I wish I could have discovered that years ago.

Drug and alcohol treatment as well as rehabilitation programs proved marginal at best for me. I went through so many outpatient programs over the years in an effort to get clean and sober. Some programs were much more intense than others, but for me, the results were negligent. I failed every time. Much of the "help" I received never worked because I knew how to play the game. I could sit in a circle all day and tell people what they wanted to hear but was out the door in no time back to drinking and/or drugging. I did parenting classes, took Antabuse, submitted to urine analyses, but none of it ever made a lasting impact on me. I think I saw most of these programs as punishments rather than true help. At one point, I flat out refused to take Antabuse or do UAs because I knew I was clean, and I didn't need to prove it to anybody but myself. Of course, that didn't impress anyone either! You can lead a horse to the trough, but you can't make it drink. I was not going to get better until I hit the very bottom of the pit. It was like I wanted to die so badly, but I just couldn't die. I needed to get past my shame and guilt so I could begin to have hope. There was only one program that helped me through my darkest hours and gave me some hope. Cenikor.

Cenikor was one very difficult program to live through, but it was a new beginning for me. I lived under the Cenikor umbrella for two and one-half years. I stayed clean and sober for that entire time, and I had to work so hard to achieve my sobriety and drug-free state. People who were not like my family surrounded me. They actually cared for me as a family should. I was taught to believe in myself, and I was given some self-esteem for the first time in my life. One did not graduate from Cenikor without an education. I got my GED while there. There was this tutor named Laverne who believed in me and would not let me give up on my GED. She was ready to move onto another job, but she stayed until I had completed my GED. The day I received my diploma, she took Princess and me out to a Mexican restaurant to celebrate my success! She knew I was smart and would not let me quit.

I celebrated the best Christmas ever while at Cenikor. There was a beautiful warm fireplace with a tree nearby all decorated up prettier than one I had ever seen. I can remember thinking that I had a family finally; people who really cared about me as a person. That Christmas, I felt like I had found a home.

The Cenikor folks called me on my poor choices and held me accountable for my choices and decisions. Black Onex and Tiger's Eye were two powerful male role models for me at Cenikor. They both saw something in me; something that, at the time, I did not even see in myself. I can remember vividly them looking at me and saying, "She's gonna make it; that girl is gonna do something with her life." I felt safe, never alone; you could not be in isolation while in Cenikor. Expectations were high for all the participants, and those expectations could be met with the support and love of the staff. I bought into the philosophy and life at Cenikor. They gave me a chance at life. I had two wonderful angels at Cenikor who stood by my side even when I later relapsed. Rubies and Opal just wouldn't give up on me. They saw potential and goodness in me; an experience I had not had hardly ever before. I don't know what it was that they thought I had, but I am forever grateful for their hope and belief in me as a human being. There was also Lauren who taught me the meaning of grace in the form of an acronym: God's riches at Christ's expense. I have never forgotten this statement. One material treasure I took with me from Cenikor was a T-shirt I made while I was there. It had a mother and daughter sitting quietly by a lake, and the saying on the shirt was "Strength comes from within." I wore this shirt for years, and it served as a reminder for me always as to where I needed to look to in order to do what I needed to do.

When I left Cenikor, I was told and expected by all to make it. I thought they had given me what I needed to make a new life without alcohol and drugs. I was so proud of all I had accomplished during the two and one-half years of being sheltered in the safe cocoon of Cenikor. I thought my family would be so proud of me and would roll out the red carpet for me when I left clean and sober. I had changed so much; I didn't realize my crazy family had not. They were the same ol' drinking partying crowd they had always been. They were not impressed with what I had figured out and accomplished during those long arduous years in Cenikor. No fanfare, no "way to go Rara," no pat on the back. Just the same old game. If you want to be around us, we are going to drink, drug, and party like always. They judged me harshly and indicated to me that now I thought I was too good for them. I was Little Miss Goody Two-Shoes.

I left my rehab with such high hopes for a new and wholesome start for my kids and me. I regained custody of both Coco and

Princess, and we were set up in a home in Lakewood, far from my family. It was me, Coco, and Princess. I had a job; I had a home; I was paying my bills. And I was terribly lonely. I have forever been so drawn to my family, and Cenikor did not prepare me for living life clean and sober on the outside of its four walls. I was so scared. I didn't know how to interact with people who didn't drink and drug. I didn't know how to act when I would take my kids to the park to play. I had never in my life done anything without alcohol and drugs. The world looked too big, too scary, and way too lonely. I was drawn back into the warmth and womb of my family. I left Cenikor in March with every intention of succeeding in my new life and with all the well-wishes and hopes from my Cenikor family. What I didn't have and what I sorely needed was a mentor from my safe haven to help me negotiate the high dark waters of real life on the outside without my trusted friends, alcohol, and crack cocaine.

When I relapsed, I did call Rubies at Cenikor in search for help, and she encouraged me to come back for group and counseling. I had failed again; I let myself down, my kids down, and I was far too embarrassed and ashamed to face the folks at Cenikor. The relapse was the worst yet, and I was the one who took back up with my previous addictions. It was not Cenikor's fault; it was all of my own choosing. I was so distraught and disappointed in myself. I didn't really have much hope of ever having a "normal" life; I had blown the best shot at the clean life that I had ever had yet.

Rehabilitation systems mean well, and they do give addicts a shot at getting better. However, the addict must want to leave his or her addictions behind them for good. Mentor programs need to be in place to help addicts survive on the outside in the real world. It is such a complex arena, and there are no easy solutions, but it must start with each individual person in order to achieve any sense of success.

Finally, the penal system is the last societal institution I experienced. Looking back, I can say that my prison experience was successful in that I never ever went back for a second round. Once I left, I never wanted to go back. As an inmate, I was frightened, and I kept it to myself. I didn't want any part of the situations in which

I found myself daily. Back when I did my time, you were allowed to wear your own clothes, smoke, and have some freedoms from the outside world. While I served my time, Corey took real good care of me making sure I had everything I could possibly need. He was a good man to stand by me during this difficult stay.

I was arrested for possessing a gun that was not mine and having Valium pills for which I did not have a prescription. The ultimate cause of my incarceration was that I failed to show up in court for my arraignment. Because I had two previous felonies on my record, I was not given another chance and was sentenced to two to four years in prison. I spent the first thirty days in the county jail before being transferred down to the Colorado Women's Correctional Facility in Canon City. In those days, they waited until there was a busload of folks before moving you down to the correctional facility because it is so far. I spent about five months in Canon City before being transferred to the halfway house on the Ft. Logan grounds. From there, I was paroled for the remainder of my sentence and was required to submit to UAs and check in with my parole officer on schedule.

Life in prison was chaotic. There were so many women all around me. They developed many lesbian relationships out of need for companionship. I had no interest in mixing with any of them and stayed as isolated as possible. There were your hard-core criminals, your knuckleheads as well as those who were not bad folks but they lacked good common sense. Inmates were required to show up on time for meals as well as work every day. I worked in the yards. We were allowed to attend church services in exchange for good behavior, and that I savored. GED tutoring, education programs, and counseling were also available to us.

The penal system is broken in many ways that outsiders never see. What goes on behind those walls is privy to those who serve time and to those who work in the prisons. Funneling of money, drugs, rape, beatings between inmates, tattooing, etc., all occur right under the prison guards' noses. They see, they hear, they just choose not to deal with the crime that exists on the inside. It is all an inside job. The reality of prison is that it is a game of survival. You do what you got to do to keep alive.

The inmates are treated like caged animals. There is little incentive to reform destructive ways of life. Prisons are warehousing people. Like most of the other systems, there are too few qualified workers to do what really needs to be done to rehabilitate the inmates. Inmates are in need of counseling and therapy. While in prison, an inmate can send a "kite" to his/her counselor or caseworker in prison concerning a problem. However, due to the overwhelming caseloads any given counselor has, it can take up to three weeks to get an appointment. By that time, it is often too late.

There is little incentive to work hard or improve one's self in prison. An inmate is paid 60 cents a day for hard labor. It is not enough to survive on in prison when you take into account what has to be purchased at the commissary. A bar of soap runs $4! If a visit to the doctor is needed, the inmate must pay to see the doctor. Family members help to support inmates while in prison. If they haven't got anybody, it is really tough to survive. Another difficulty is many inmates are ordered to pay restitution for their crimes. That's a difficult feat to achieve on 60 cents a day. It is overwhelming and dehumanizing; it is not an incentive to do better. Many inmates just do their time and survive. They never work at improving their lives because it is not a valued thing to do. The penal system needs to work on a solution for how to get these people out of jail and keep them out of jail.

When I left prison, I never wanted to go back. While on parole, I did have a dirty UA, and my parole officer gave me a choice: go back to prison or enter into an intense twenty-one-day program to get myself clean. He gave me a valued chance, and I took it. I think the prison system is most broken when people are not given a second chance or an opportunity to make things right. My prison number is a five-digit number. It is forever with me, and I will never forget it.

I have learned many difficult lessons via all these systems. I have some sense of what works well and what doesn't. Being on the inside makes one view societal systems differently and with experienced perspectives. I know all the above-mentioned institutions are in place to try and help people like me, but there are too many folks who are running them who have lost their own perspective about what is good or not good for others. Some are on power trips and love being in control of others' lives. People need help, compassion, and real-life skills and tools to survive this cold, harsh world. Building self-esteem, providing education and genuine hope are essential aspects of providing new beginnings to those who don't know how to live in a world without addictive substances. Passing judgment and not holding people accountable for life choices perpetuates the broken lives of people.

BLUE DENIM OVERALLS
FLOATING AMONGST
SOOTHING BILLOWS
OF COTTON

L abor Day weekend of 1996 was the beginning of the end of the very long struggle with my drug and alcohol addictions. My addictions would haunt me for a couple more years before I finally surrendered, but this was where the end of the dark devastating tunnel would become somewhat closer. I would lose my Coco to suicide, and I would very nearly lose my own life as a result of the horrific events of this holiday weekend.

To recap, I had left Cenikor, clean and sober, in March 1995. I won custody of both of my children, and we settled in Lakewood with our new life. However, my addictions came back to claim me once again on Thanksgiving Day of 1995. Coco was a senior in high school and would be graduating in May 1996. As my drugging and alcohol took over my life once again, I quit my job in April 1996 so I could smoke crack cocaine full time. I had paid for Coco's graduation fees, gotten his senior pictures taken, so I felt like I had taken care of all my responsibilities with my son. Princess had begun to have fun running and playing in the neighborhood, so in my mind, my smoking crack cocaine didn't seem to be hurting anybody. Of course, by August, Social Services took Princess away again which should have been a wake-up call.

On the Friday of Labor Day weekend of 1996, little out of the norm was happening for me. I was smoking dope all day but ran out. I called up Lucinda, my boyfriend Paul's sister, for more dope. She was a tweaker and a dealer. I went to her house to buy my dope. There was an old man sitting at Lucinda's dining table; he was about sixty years old. I had never seen him before. He didn't say anything to me, nor did I have anything to say to him. I just wanted to get my dope and head back home. However, she enlisted my help in helping her clean her kitchen stove since she was moving out to her new Section 8 housing on Monday. I have always been a good house-keeper since Nanny had taught me so well, and I didn't mind lending a hand. That woman's stove was beyond bad and gross. I spent quite a lot of time getting her stove clean.

When I was done, I went to pay for my dope and head back home. However, I found that my dope money in my wallet was gone. Somebody had stolen my money while I was cleaning that damn stove. I threw quite a fit, but of course, nobody owned up to stealing my money. Lucinda and her future son-in-law offered to take me home in an effort to calm me down. I had no way to prove anyone had taken my money, so I accepted the ride home. I was sitting in the backseat of the car, and Lucinda was passed out in the front seat of the car as her future son-in-law drove. Her purse was sitting on the console between the driver and Lucinda, and I simply helped myself to the food stamps, a blank check, and $20.00 found in her purse. Someone in her house had stolen my money, so I was just paying myself back. If the young man driving saw me do it, he never said a word. I arrived home safe and sound around seven or eight Saturday night, just without my dope.

Sunday was always beer day. I walked to the store and bought a 40-ounce bottle of beer. Coco was out doing his thing, and I was just enjoying my Sunday with beer. I was preparing myself for my meeting with Rubies from Cenikor on Tuesday. I needed to get myself off crack cocaine and get Princess back. Lucinda and her girlfriend, Bonnie, showed up at my house unannounced that Sunday. Lucinda asked me if she could borrow some Chore Boy as she was out. Chore Boy is used in smoking a crack-cocaine pipe; it serves as a filter in the pipe. I went upstairs in my room to get her some Chore Boy as I never left any of my drug paraphernalia anywhere but my bedroom because of the kids. While I was upstairs, they slipped something into my beer. I gave them the Chore Boy, and they left thinking I was going to be a dead woman because they had tainted my beer. After they left, I took a swig of my beer; I thought it just tasted bad for some reason, so I threw the rest of it out. They had tried to do something to me at this time but were unsuccessful. I suspected nothing; I just brushed it off thinking I had gotten a bad bottle of beer.

That Sunday afternoon, Lucinda started calling me asking if I would come back to help her with the packing of the house. She called multiple times hoping I would agree to come over, telling me she was working on finding me a ride to her house. Later that evening, Clyde, a friend of Lucinda, showed up to take me to her house. I am such a sucker and don't hold grudges, so I was happy to go help. I did not entertain the possibility that Lucinda might have other motives for me to come to her house. Clyde just dropped me off and left. The old man was at the table again with a liter of liquor in front of him and tried to get me to drink some of it. I wasn't interested because I was hoping for some dope from Lucinda. She called me into her bedroom to come and get some dope, which I was happy to do; it would make our work more fun and lighter! I went into the kitchen to get a beer as I was gearing up for packing up the house. Next, I hollered at Lucinda to find out which room she wanted to start in.

The next event should have alerted me to something not being quite as it would seem. Bonnie showed up at Lucinda's front door very early Sunday morning, and those two women had quite a fight. They were yelling and screaming at each other over something. The two of them are rarely apart, and it seemed odd that they would be having such a terrible falling out, especially at that time of the morning. Lucinda went into her room and slammed the door while Bonnie came into the kitchen, grabbed a beer out of the fridge and slammed that door before she left out the front door. They were snarling angry women!

The next thing I know, Lucinda comes into the kitchen saying she wants to get some breakfast before we start packing. She had not eaten all day, and she needed some food to calm her down after the fight. When doing drugs and alcohol, you have to eat periodically to keep your addictions going right. So I didn't really care if we went to eat instead of packing; I was just there to try to help.

I never saw it coming. I guess after all these years of people taking advantage of me, I hadn't learned that things might not be as they appear. Lucinda drove the car; I sat in the front seat while the old man was in the back. We drove past the Village Inn, but she just kept on driving saying that we should go up to Central City and have some fun. Next thing she said was that there was this friend of hers who lived in Golden whom she thought I would really like, so maybe we should go pick him up first to go with us to Central City. So much for getting breakfast! We were heading up to Golden on a dark two-lane road. We were in the middle of nowhere. Lucinda stopped the car and reached for something under her front seat before she got out; she said she had to pee. All of a sudden, she tears open my car door and points a gun at my head saying, "Bitch, this is where you die tonight!" She pulled the trigger, and the first bullet grazed my right temple. I was so scared; I didn't know what was going to happen to me.

I tried to get out of the car while holding my bleeding head. I was stunned! The old man got out next, and I thought he was going to help me. He came up behind me and began stabbing me over and over again with a fingernail file. He just started ripping at my skin on my neck, my head, and my back. He was going to skin me alive! I started to run with nowhere to go. There was nothing but highway in front of me, a big hill on my right and a drop into a ravine on my left. I headed down the hill, slipping and sliding all the while. I could hear the gun firing and them chasing after me. Lucinda shot me five times before I heard the gun ring out with empty clicks. The old man kept coming on me, plucking and plucking at me wherever he could. I tried to cover my head with my hands to protect myself, but he just kept at it. They had me cornered at the bottom of the ravine near a fence made out of something like chicken wire. I fell to the ground, crying and begging them to stop. They stood over me, kicking me and plucking at me with that damn nail file. Lucinda kept pulling the trigger of the empty gun while aiming it at my head. I was completely helpless in the middle of nowhere with two crazy and cruel people torturing and taunting me. Finally, I quit fighting and lay nearly dead. I stopped breathing and lost consciousness. Lucinda thought she had finally killed me, and they left satisfied that they had done what they had been trying to do for two days.

I drifted in and out of consciousness. I just lay there dying, and I remember thinking this was it. It was warm even though I had on only a T-shirt, pants, and my rundown ol' tennis shoes. I had no jacket. For a cool September night, I couldn't get over how warm it was. I just wanted to stay there and let go of my tragic life. There was no reason to keep doing what I was doing, even the thought of Coco and Princess were not enough to make me want to live.

As I lay there, I saw my life flash in front of me. It was like a movie projector telling the story of my life. The most striking memory of this experience is that there was absolutely nothing good going on in that movie. All I saw were the bad parts of my life; there was nothing good to hold onto. It was such a vivid movie and so terribly sad. Looking back, I realize now that I didn't see anything good because all my life I had chosen bad. I wanted to just let go and die. But that scared me too!

I began to pray to God asking Him to help me. I promised Him I would get myself clean and stay clean if He would just help me out of this situation. Seems like I turn to God only in my most desperate hour. It was so dark; there were no lights, no nothing, just pitch-black. I began to notice myself floating amongst soft billows of cotton, being rocked back and forth in their softness and warmth. A pair of blue denim overalls hovered over me, and I heard Big Daddy's strong voice. He said, "Get up, Baby Girl, get up!" The voice was so clear and present that I knew I had to respond. Big Daddy had come to help me.

I began to drag myself up out of that ravine. I crawled up the dry dirt as far as my strength would carry me and would slide back down the ravine. There was nothing to grab onto or to dig my shoes into on the dry hillside. Once again, I lay there in the warmth just ready to give up, and Big Daddy's voice would ring in my head, "Come on, Baby Girl. You can do this. Get up!" I struggled up three different times before I made it out of the ravine. When I finally neared the top, I grabbed hold of a utility pole and pulled myself up by the road. I couldn't move. I saw the headlights of a lone car coming down the road. I picked up a stick that I found lying next to me and waved it. The car stopped. A man got out of the car and came to my side. Another car stopped, and the driver was a woman; she was a paramedic. They called 911, and an ambulance came to my rescue. I was on the verge of dying. The man had just gotten off duty; he worked for the Jefferson County Sheriffs Department. It was so dark on that lonely road that it was hard to see anything. He said he thought my stick was a deer antler, and he had stopped so as not to hit the deer. The paramedic was kind and gentle as she whispered to me that everything was going to be okay. I cried and asked her if I was going to die. Once the ambulance arrived and began to stabilize me on the stretcher, I became so very cold. I shivered and shook; the warmth of the cotton billows had left me as did the floating denim overalls.

I was taken to St. Anthony's Central Hospital where I was admitted to the ICU. They had to cut my clothes from my body; they were torn and imbedded in my sliced skin. The caring hands of the doctors and nurses put me back together. When I arrived at the hospital early Monday morning, I was able to describe what had happened to me and who had attacked me. I told the whole story truthfully about how I had stolen from Lucinda's purse, what I had taken, the awful tasting beer, the old man who tried to skin me alive, and the gun that had been used to shoot me. By noon on Labor Day, the police had arrested all those who had tried to kill me including Lucinda, Bonnie, the old man, and Clyde. They found everything just as I had said including the food stamps and the blank check. I had spent the $20 on my beer. When they pulled up to Lucinda's house, they found the whole lot of those crazy, violent people celebrating my destruction and death. The gun was never found, so Lucinda was able to plead to lesser charges. All served time for their attack on me. Clyde was charged with getting rid of the evidence and Bonnie for being an accomplice. Lucinda got seventeen years, and the old man was sentenced to twelve years. Lucinda's sentence was harsher because she had a felony record; she had done something similar to her husband less than a year before. Had the gun been found, I believe she would have received forty-eight years to life for her crime against me.

While in the hospital, my brother Capt'n came to see me. He didn't really care about what had happened to me; he just want to know where Princess was. He started immediately to work on gaining custody of her once again. I don't remember anyone really much caring about me fighting for my life other than my Cenikor family. They continued to have compassion for me in my dire situation.

When I came home, Coco was my caregiver once again. My sweet son made a bed for me in the living room until I was able to make it up the stairs again. I remember feeling pleased that I had made it home in time to celebrate Coco's eighteenth birthday. We had a regular party with ice cream and cake. However, the celebration didn't last long. I sank into a deep depression after the attack, especially when it came time for the testifying about what had happened to me. I dug myself into a deep, dark hole where nobody could reach me or hurt me ever again. Life was too hard, and nothing felt safe, not even Coco. My drugs and alcohol were the only trusted friends I could count on. I slipped deeper and deeper into my addictions. Coco begged me to stop smoking crack cocaine. He suggested I do pot as it was not nearly as damaging as crack cocaine. But I couldn't get high on pot. I remember yelling at him one night, telling him to get the hell out of my life. I had to do what I had to do. I remember so well my son crying that night. It was the only time I ever remember him crying, tears rolling down his beautiful face, mainly because of the harsh words I had spoken to him.

After the attack, I was faced with the legal ramifications of what had happened to me. I was able to take the District Attorney to the exact spot where I had been stabbed and shot. My blood was there at the bottom of that ravine; I relived every moment of that nightmare. Lucinda's mother called numerous times begging me not to testify against her daughter. She said Lucinda's children needed her, that she was a good person, and that she would give me anything I wanted if I would just not testify against Lucinda. She made me feel guilty for filing assault charges against the woman who had tried so very hard to murder me. It was all too much for me to cope with and endure.

I didn't keep my promise to God. I failed Coco miserably. I was too embarrassed to face my Cenikor family. Life was too damn hard; I wondered why I had tried so hard to climb out of that ravine. I later lost Coco in November to suicide. Maybe my life was too much for him to carry as well. It took two more years for me to bury myself so deep in a hole where I knew I would die if I didn't surrender my addictions.

How could I have survived five-gunshot wounds and innumerable stabbings and return to my beloved addictions? How could I sacrifice my own son for my selfishness? How could I face myself in a mirror ever again once I had lost my son? I guess God never gives up on us and is willing to take us back any time we are ready. I have severe scars to remind myself every day of my attack, my son, my poor life choices. But my scars also remind me of how in the end, I gave my heart to my Lord and found His forgiveness and His love for this sinner. God loves me; He guides me; He has saved me in this life and the next.

Because of this horrific attack, I began to find angels, quiet unassuming angels, who had compassion for me. They did not judge me. They saw goodness and potential in me that no one else ever saw. They believed in me, and they gave me a chance to let go of my lousy addictions and find a new way of life without drugs and alcohol. They held me up and showed me the way to live life without drugs and alcohol. They allowed me to develop self-esteem and self-value and worth. They began to open doors to opportunities that I believed could be mine if I just wanted them bad enough. They offered me education, hope, and love when even my family never thought I deserved those precious gifts. My angels helped me flourish and blossom enough to gain custody of Princess for one last time.

I know my whole life has been mostly wasted on substance abuse. It nearly cost me my own life, and it did cost me the life of my son. But the Labor Day weekend of 1996 had a silver lining in that I began to face what I wanted my scars to represent to me. I chose a life I never dreamt possible, and I think my Coco would be proud of what his mother finally chose. All Coco ever wanted from me was to be clean and sober so he could be with me.

THE LONG JOURNEY BACK

My attack was a horrible experience, but it was the beginning of me finding my way out of my self-destruction. My crack-cocaine and alcohol addictions did not subside for two more years, but I began to meet people who had compassion for me and who would offer me help I had not received before. Because of this violent crime that had been committed against me, I think people saw me in a different light. A person who was from the Victim's Advocate program was assigned to see me. I received counseling and therapy on a whole new level. The Jeffco Advocacy program was willing to pay for my treatment and medications and helped me keep my doctors' appointments. They made sure I received the required procedures such as my MRIs. However, I was scared for my health and myself more than I had ever been in my entire life. I was also more overwhelmed with life than ever before. I soon found solace only through smoking my crack cocaine and drinking my booze.

Christmas 1996 was one of the best Princess and I ever experienced as far as presents. The District Attorney's office and Human Services provided us with more than we could possibly have wished for; it was an amazing Christmas. We were a part of the Adopt-A-Family Program, and we were given more than we had ever hoped for.

These wonderful angels were like invisible Santa Clauses granting our every wish. It was a Christmas I will never forget.

My life was complicated even further with the loss of Coco. I didn't have it in me to fight enough to gain custody of Princess. I was in a wilderness of drugs and alcohol, and I had no way of getting out or wanting to find my way out. I was back to my old tricks as far as showing up for Princess. When it came time for our visits, I was often absent. I was too drunk or too high to deal with my daughter. I would call to say I needed more time to get myself together or that I was not ready yet. On the inside, I saw myself as useless and selfish. I just couldn't show up for this kid. I was doing to Princess what I had done to Coco for years and years. I would see myself in the mirror and see all those ugly scars; I was reminded of what Sweets had said over and over again. I was no good. I would never amount to anything; I was ugly and worthless. When I smoked dope or drank booze, I couldn't see any of those things in the mirror.

I was assigned to a psychiatrist because of my accident. This therapy proved to be of little help; I had heard it all before. I knew what I needed to do; I just wasn't ready to do it. They assigned a lady to come to my house to check in with me and to hold therapy sessions in my home. I'd see her coming, and out the back door I would go. I knew she would take a UA sample, and damn, I didn't need her to tell me it was dirty; I already knew that. The bottom line was that I didn't want to be here anymore; I was done living. I tried so hard to do myself in through drugs and alcohol, but it just wasn't happening. No matter how much dope I smoked or how much I drank, I simply could not die. That is a horrible thing when you try to die, and you just can't! I just never got that lucky.

In December of 1997, I received my settlement from Social Security for my attack. I got $5,300. I thought I would use it to get myself an apartment and a new life. I chose to drug and drink instead. I went through every penny in three weeks. I went from having the most money I had ever had at one time to being completely homeless and on the streets in three short weeks. I remained homeless until the following June.

I lived in the shelters and in hotels on east Colfax, working day labor jobs to support myself. I'd get enough to pay the hotel bill for three weeks at a time, but before I knew it, the three weeks would be up, and I'd be looking for ways to pay for a place to lay my head at night again.

I was able to hook up with new and old friends during this time. I met a woman at my day labor job that came to stay with me in my hotel room for a few days. She was trying to get rid of her husband. When she drank, she would become promiscuous, and he did not like it one bit. Why is okay for a man to come onto a woman when he drinks, but a drinking woman cannot show any "unacceptable" behaviors? Women are held to a different standard! She let me borrow her car. I drove it around for a few days before it quit on me in Montebello; the starter went out. I had to leave the damn car there until I could hustle and panhandle enough money to fix the starter that had broken on me. My family accused me of stealing that car and gave me no help. I hitched a ride back into Denver with a guy I had never met before. We got pulled over; he was arrested and taken to jail for a DUI and having no license. As for me, the first of many angels had arrived on the scene. The "good cops," that is what I called them, decided to take me to Denver Cares rather than anywhere else as I had not broken any law. I arrived at Denver Cares, a detox place, with a pint of vodka and a package of cigarettes on my person; that was it. This is where I finally surrendered. At the end when the music finally stopped, I decided if I couldn't die on crack cocaine, I might as well try to live without it.

I met with a nurse there and begged her to help me. I couldn't face going back out on the streets again. I remember telling her if she recommended that I go back out there, I would die. I was not good at being a homeless person. It was not a lifestyle I could face again. I told her I could not live like this anymore. For whatever reason, this dear sweet woman truly listened to me; she heard me. She allowed me to stay at Denver Cares until a spot opened up at the Salvation Army. She was my first savior.

Salvation Army continued the hard work I had begun at Cenikor. Salvation Army provides lots of structure to addicts like me. Structure was exactly what I needed if I was to beat my addictions. I found angels everywhere I looked. These people welcomed me and cared about me as a human being. They were compassionate and loving, and they believed in me. I had experienced much of the same at Cenikor. The difference between the programs was that Cenikor was therapeutic based whereas Salvation Army was faith based. I was ready to surrender my heart to God.

I stayed at Cottonwood, which is the place Salvation Army provides for women. There are three rules one must abide by while staying at the Salvation Army. You must have a case manager who provides you treatment; you must go to church, and you must attend NA (Narcotics Anonymous), AA (Alcoholics Anonymous), or CA (Cocaine Anonymous) while in the program. These mandatory rules helped me stay on the straight and narrow. I was required to work in the stinky warehouses eight hours a day, picking through smelly, old donated clothes to pay for my stay at Cottonwood where I received food, shelter, and treatment. We were bused over there every morning and supervised by the "Sally Police" while on the job. There were no outside jobs. I was kept busy living rather than kept busy dying like before. I worked like I never had before at getting myself clean and sober. I began to live.

When I first arrived to Cottonwood, I received help and advice from my big sister, Rose. She, too, was a client at Cottonwood but had just been there a little longer than I. She helped me learn the ropes of the place so that I could adjust more quickly and become more comfortable in my new home. We attended my AA meetings together. I remember the hot June day when Rose and I attended our first AA meeting. The van from Cottonwood dropped us off for the meeting, and I had $8 in my pocket. The place where the AA meeting was held was across the street from a Safeway. Next to the Safeway was a liquor store. Rose had to run into Safeway before the meeting to buy some Pepsi. I waited outside for her, and then we would go into the meeting together. I remember this day because it was the first day I made a conscious choice not to go into that liquor store and buy me a nice tall cold can of beer. I wanted it so bad that I trembled, but I didn't do it. And I had $8 in my pocket, but I didn't give into my profound desire for a beer; that was a monumental day for me!

I had attended AA meetings before, but this was the first time I truly wanted to be there. There was this long, unending hallway with people everywhere I looked. There were wall-to-wall people, and they were so welcoming and made me feel comfortable. I can remember being so nervous when I was dropped off by the van. I didn't tell my story that day, but I told my name and said I was very glad to be there. I can remember a feeling of being saved and rescued that day. What a relief and joy! I had tears running down my face because I was beginning my long journey back from my addictions. It felt so good.

The more I attended my AA meetings, the more I admired the folks who were there. There were these six men who between them had two hundred years of sobriety; that's living success and hope for someone like me! After an AA meeting one day, we were coming out, and a woman whom I had never seen before, pulled up in her car, got out, and gave me a book. It was called *God's Calling*. She just came out of nowhere. I asked my housemother, Rose, if I could keep the book. She looked it over and said it was a good book for me to have. This book has helped me over and over again. I read it every morning with my Bible. It is a book of simple readings that gives me daily meditations, something to focus on for the day. That was one of God's first winks for me. He reached out to me through this total stranger and gave me a gift I will treasure forever.

I was working hard at Cottonwood learning how to live life without drugs and alcohol. For the first time, I began to feel the pain and sorrow of my life and face up to the consequences of my choices. On September 10, Coco's twentieth birthday, I remember rising for work at the warehouse. It was a bright, sunny day, and I was ready to embrace another hardworking day sorting through those smelly clothes. We were riding in the van to work, and I can remember passing two different trucks delivering alcohol to who knows where. I could tell they were alcohol trucks because of the advertisements displayed on the outsides of the trucks. I wanted a drink so bad I could have cried. When I got to the warehouse, I was suddenly completely overwhelmed with life, and I just couldn't face sorting those damn clothes. I told the supervisor that I had to speak with someone, anyone, before I could begin to work that day. The supervisor called Black Diamond, the Director of Services at the Salvation Army, came to see me. Black Diamond had a shiny baldhead, wore a bowtie, and looked like the nutty professor, but this man listened to me. He didn't just brush me off as a crazy woman who didn't want to do her job that day. He listened. I will never forget this day either. It was a huge breakthrough for me in understanding what life was handing out to me. As I met with Black Diamond, I cried uncontrollably and just couldn't stop. I told him it was Coco's birthday and how I had lost my beloved son. Black Diamond explained to me that I was finally grieving the death of my son, and I was feeling the full force of that horrific pain because I was clean and sober. Rather than forcing me to work my shift as required by the rules, he allowed me to go to the chapel and sit all morning just to cry. It was a cleansing cry, and some healing began to take place in me like I had never experienced before. It felt so good, yet it was so terribly painful to actually feel on that level. I was able to return to the warehouse by noon and finish my shift. Black Diamond allowed me to feel. He knew that was far more important than sorting smelly clothes. Black Diamond had compassion for me. It wasn't about the production or the rules; it was about not losing the person. Black Diamond was my kind, gentle giant of a man; his face will always be with me.

I thrived on the church services we were allowed to attend. Raw Gold and his beautiful wife, Jewel, were instrumental in my meeting God in a way I had never imagined. They led the midweek services as well as the Sunday school. Between hearing the scriptures anew and singing songs of love and praise, my soul soared. I found such calm and solace when I attended services. I was getting high on the love of the Lord and not on drugs or booze.

Jewel met with me often, one-on-one, and would read to me from the Bible. I heard for the first time how much God loved me and how He knew me even when I was in my mother's womb. He knew each and every hair on my head, my head! What a remarkable God I was discovering; One who loved me for who I was and not One who had condemned me to hell for all the bad things I had done in my life. My thirst for the word of God was being quenched while, at the same time, I just couldn't hear enough!

Raw Gold and Jewel encouraged me to sing as loud as I could. I thrived on songs like "Amazing Grace" and "Soon, Very Soon, We're Going to See the King." The words to my Precious Lord made my heart light with joy and delight. The more I fell in love with my

God, the louder I would sing. Jewel always greeted me with a warm smile and a generous heart. She told me to use my strong, deep voice to praise the Lord for all He had given me. She gave me permission to be who I wanted to be, and she never judged me harshly because I longed to sing from the mountaintop about my love for the Lord. Such a new concept of God! So different than the God I was taught about from Nanny and Grandmother Macey. My burden was becoming lighter with each passing day. I was beginning to live for the first time ever, and what joy I felt!

Jewel gave me several bookmarks reminding me of God's love and goodness. I have kept every single one as well as every song sheet given at each service I attended. Those words gave me such hope for the new life I was beginning to live. I received my Bible at Salvation Army, and I read it every single day. I was learning how to open myself up to Jesus, and all surrendering of my past life and myself happened at this blessed Salvation Army.

I met many of my earthly angels while at Salvation Army. People there actually cared about me, and they were so nonjudgmental. I learned how to trust people and began to open to those who wanted me to learn to really live life to its fullest. I have mentioned Black Diamond, Raw Gold, and Jewel, but there were still others. Amethyst was my case manager. She was the first person in my life I think I really trusted. She listened and heard me. I had a feeling of being safe and cared for when I was with her. While at Cottonwood, she headed up several groups such as drug and alcohol workshops. I remember the day she asked me to tell her one of my deepest, darkest secrets, something I had never told another person. I found I could tell her, and she was accepting, not shocked. She simply asked me how I felt about what I had told her. There was no condescension or judgment; she allowed me to feel some cleansing and calm in being able to share my secrets with her.

Garnett taught me to read from Proverbs every day to help me manage my anger. My anger-management classes were taught by Garnett, and I still practice the skills she gave me. I am able to find something in Proverbs every day to help ease my pain.

I longed to identify with a family. I yearned for family, a true and loving family. I wanted a family who could love me for who I was and who I was becoming. Salvation Army was recapping for me all that I had learned at Cenikor, but they tapped into the power I held as a good person and helped me learn to use that power to defeat my addictions once and for all. Cenikor had helped me clean up my act, but Salvation Army gave me the life skills and belief system to help me stay clean and sober. It is such a long, difficult journey! Faith in God has proven to be the ticket for me to continue on my road to successful living.

I graduated from Cottonwood in December of 1998. I came out of the Salvation Army with some skills I had not gained at Cenikor a few years earlier. It provided me with the structure and the mentors I needed to learn how to survive outside their safe and comforting walls. There was an aftercare plan where I was encouraged to stay clean and sober. It also included the twelve-step plan which has proven so successful with many addicts. Once I left the safe walls of Cottonwood, it took me a few months to actually enter into the twelve-step AA plan. I had to return to the hood where people knew my past and me. They knew of my numerous attempts to get clean and sober as well of my continuous failures. But when I got there and I was ready to accept the genuine help available to me, I never looked back.

When I left Salvation Army in December of 1998, I moved in with my brother Capt'n so I could be close to Princess. Those eleven months proved to be a true test of my dedication and determination to stay my clean and sober course. Capt'n smoked cigarettes and pot as well as consuming alcohol daily while I lived in his house. In a way, he taunted me with these vices, but I turned away from the temptations so that I could gain custody of my daughter. There were so many difficult minutes, hours, and days; times when I do not know how I continued toward my goals. Princess was a pawn used by my brother to keep control of me. There were so many days I longed for a drink, a hit, a place of my own. I survived by joining a church close by and attending my AA meetings, participating in the twelve-step plan. Church took up lots of my time.

I met my next earthly angel at the Stout Street Foundation. Her name was Short Stuff. She looked like something straight out of the hippie days. As I think of it, all the folks who worked at Stout Street had the hippie look! Short Stuff was kind and gentle, and she too listened to me, really listened. She supported me during those eleven months, offering advice and options to living with Capt'n. Just having someone to talk with and someone who allowed me to even think of options made all the difference in the world. I never felt trapped amid. I was strengthened by her encouragement. I could have real control of my choices and life. Short Stuff believed in me!

During this time, I continued to receive support from my social-security income. Short Stuff was in charge of my money. It would be deposited in my bank account, but I needed to go through Short Stuff in order to get to my funds. I found it very helpful to have her involved in my handling of money. She was teaching me how to budget and pay my bills on time. I always had the rent ready and available to pay Capt'n when the time came. These were new skills I had the opportunity to learn via Short Stuff.

After living with Capt'n for eleven months, Short Stuff helped me find a one-bedroom apartment. I had to continue to prove to the Social Services that I could indeed stay clean and sober as well as demonstrate my ability to provide a stable home for Princess. Short Stuff also helped me compose my letter to the probate court in my effort to win my daughter back from Capt'n.

While staying with Capt'n, I began to work toward becoming a certified addiction counselor through Vocational Rehabilitation Services. I had started the process once before, and I wanted more than anything else to help others who were addicts like me. I wanted to be to others what those at Cenikor and Cottonwood had been to me. The certification requires three thousand hours of classes and training; I had earned one thousand hours just from my time spent at Cenikor. Due to my past record of failing to follow through on my previous commitment to rehab, I had to prove to Voc Rehab that I was serious this time.

I submitted to UAs to prove my sobriety and drug-free status during the training. I had already been clean and sober for well over a year at this point, and I was determined to gain my certification as a counselor.

There was an angel who lived next door to Capt'n. Esther helped me do what I had to do. No matter how upset and frustrated I would get living at my brother's house, she would remind me I had to stay in the race. She would not let me give up believing that Princess was worth the difficult times I was experiencing. Esther also helped me with Princess's care. If I were going to be late coming home from my appointments at Stout Street or the Choosing Life Center where I was taking my classes, she would have Princess come to her house. There were times when I just couldn't make it back in time due to class and bus schedules. This dear sweet grandmother took Princess and me to church with her. She belonged to one of the big mega-churches. When I left to continue to live on my own while waiting to prove myself to the system, Capt'n would allow her to take Princess with her to church. At times, I would hook up with them there.

I attended drug and alcohol classes at the Choosing Life Center. Choosing Life Center was a facility connected with the Stout Street Foundation. A lady at the center took an interest in me; we had many talks about this wonderful book *Conversations with God*. This book had a huge impact on my conversion process, and she too had a similar experience with the book. Carolyn ended up becoming my mentor for several years. In many ways, she was like the mother I never had. She was genuinely kind and warm. She listened to me, and she coached me in life. She was my angel of peace. I never felt judged by her; I found I could be open and honest with her always. I learned many helpful parenting tips from her; she calmed my fears about my capability of becoming a good and competent mother to Princess. Carolyn encouraged me to lead drug and alcohol groups at the Stout Street Foundation as my training progressed. She saw in me what other people did not see.

Carolyn taught me about the reality of relationships. When various events would come up and she was not able to keep our dinner dates or appointments, I would feel anxious and sometimes abandoned by her. I grew up and matured under Carolyn's guidance and love. She taught me that things happen in life, and that was just the way it was. Sometimes situations are unavoidable. It didn't mean I was not cared for or valued.

I remember Carolyn would ask me what I was goin' to do when she could not be there some day. I learned to accept that people can't be with me always and that nobody can define the length of time we get to spend together. Relationships are but a season long, and that's all you get.

Carolyn died in February 2008 after a long battle with breast cancer. It was beyond difficult to lose my mentor, my friend. But I attended her funeral, and I was there to say good-bye. I am still moving forward, being responsible and doing what a grown woman is supposed to do. I miss my guardian angel, my angel who loved and nurtured me like no other human being ever has.

When Carolyn got sick and had to leave due to her chemo treatments, the Choosing Life Center closed. Carolyn's ex-husband, Brad, ran the Stout Street Foundation. He had heard about my life's story and me. He took a chance on me and allowed me to come to the clinic to finish my internship that I had begun at the Choosing Life Center. Several of the staff members did not care for the different counseling techniques I used with my groups. Stout Street was a much looser organization than what I had experienced at Cenikor or Cottonwood. I brought the Cenikor-style to Stout Street because I felt these techniques were far more effective in dealing with addicts. Several of the staff tried to get rid of me, but Brad told them I was going nowhere. He stood up for me, and I ended up staying for two and a half years. Brad was an unconventional kind of guy, but he cared for people, and he had a big heart.

Violet was the next angel to come into my life. Princess was ten or eleven. One day when she went to school, she told her teacher that she had a dream in which she stabbed herself repeatedly because she had lost her brother. She needed to be with her brother. A social worker was called in, and Princess was taken to the hospital for evaluation. It was suggested that Princess participate in a program known as the mobile crisis. Therapists come to the home and do counseling on site. It began as family counseling for Princess and me and eventually developed into individual counseling for each of us.

From there, we were connected with Mental Health Services of Colorado, and our counseling continued. Princess improved with each session. We learned how to communicate better, and we began to come back together. I had won Princess back from my brother, and I would not lose her ever again. I was determined to do whatever it took to keep my daughter with me, and I wanted us to develop a strong relationship. It would take lots of counseling, patience, and love on both our parts to succeed. I have had Princess with me now for ten years.

Violet was our therapist, and she was one hell of a therapist! She was such a good listener. She heard what I was really saying; my words did not fall on deaf ears. Violet helped me to understand what Carolyn had been trying to teach me for so many years. People come and go in your life; they are not always going to be there. It is unrealistic to think anyone will always be there. I learned I had to allow people to move on; this includes my daughter when the time comes. If I ever finish my degree in counseling, I want to be a therapist just like her; she listened! Violet told me I have all the answers I need to live my life well; I just need to bring those out and have the faith and confidence in myself to believe what I know already is right.

There were two other very important angels that came in and out of my life over this long journey. As a matter of fact, these two women are my best buddies still. I first met them while I was at Cenikor. I was in the twelve-step AA program, and they sponsored me in this program. They were like my pillars of hope, and when I relapsed in 1995, Salt and Pepper didn't desert me or judge me for failing. They simply encouraged me to return to the twelve-step program. When Coco died, who came to his funeral to show how much they cared about my horrific loss and me? Salt and Pepper. I could easily understand these women. They were no-nonsense kind of people who tell it like it is. Neither woman ever quits, even when it seems impossible to go on. Pepper is determined to nurse this world back to health, and Salt is supporting her every inch of the way. These two earthly angels have given me unconditional love for so long that my life would not be as complete without them. I am forever grateful to my buddies.

REFLECTIONS ON MY LIFE

I am no longer ashamed of being me. I am not a quitter. No matter how many times I tried to give up my alcohol and drug addictions and failed to do so, I never gave up. Today I am not the broken vessel of a woman I once was, nor am I completely healed or whole. Every day I do all I can to remember that I have been given a second chance on life, and I try to make each and every day count. I start every day with prayer and ask for the courage and guidance to give my best to all I encounter. I try to remember not to be afraid; I can face my fears and do not allow them to control my life.

I have begun to watch for the various "winks from God" that come my way to help me live life more fully. One has to watch for those winks, and when they come, embrace them as the gifts from God that they are. I received many gifts while at the Stout Street Foundation, including the courage to dream and find ways to make those dreams come true. With Short Stuff's help, I learned how to manage my money and realize that I did not have to spend every dime I earned. She helped me begin to save my money so that I could become a homeowner. It took me two years, but I was able to save $2,000 for the down payment for my condo. In November 2004, I became a homeowner for the first time. Princess and I had a place of our own. I celebrated having a mortgage payment. I am the first of my family's cousins to own my very own place.

I also began to clean up the wreckage that I had created when I relapsed after Cenikor. I paid off all my credit-card debt, and I learned to live on little. I never needed to buy the most expensive things on the store shelves. As long as it was clean and it fit, I was content to buy those clothes. I taught Princess that sacrifices needed to be made in order to make our dreams happen. We ate a lot of pizza in those days.

Princess and I had to rely on public transportation to do everything we needed to do. We would walk several blocks to the grocery store and push the grocery buggy home through the snow in order to get our food home. We took the RTD and light rail everywhere, oftentimes having to transfer multiple times to get where we needed to go. In 2002 when I was able to buy my very first car, I was forty-two years old. It was a sixteen-year-old Honda Civic that I nicknamed "Jesus" as it had a symbol of Jesus on the back of the car. Our lives changed dramatically as a result of that car. I was beginning to make good things happen in my life, and I felt so good. No more "buggy pushing" in the snow!

I opened a legal checking account. This too was a huge help to my budgeting and paying bills. Before this time, I would drag Princess with me to the post office and have to purchase money orders to pay each and every bill. Having a simple checking account made our lives so much better. I realized that to many people owning a home, a car and having a checking account is just part of life. But for me, they are symbols of hope and dreams that I thought I would never have. I have learned to take nothing for granted. Each is a blessing to my beautiful daughter and me.

I worked at the Stout Street Foundation as an addiction counselor for two and one-half years. While working there, I received an unexpected phone call from a gal who worked at Empowerment. They were in need of an addiction counselor for their pretreatment and outreach programs. I was once told one reason I have been as successful as I have been as a counselor is because I have walked the walk for the alcohol and crack-cocaine addicts I advise. I know their pain and sorrow. I know how hard it is to become clean and sober and stay that way. I know the storm in their lives firsthand.

I knew of the Empowerment Program from my own experience. White Diamond came to the Colorado Women's Correction Center in Canon City when I was an inmate.

I was accepted into her program in 1988. I was able to get a job working at a factory in downtown Denver as a result of the help I received from Empowerment. So when White Diamond at Empowerment offered me a job interview, I was delighted! After the interview, White Diamond and I reminisced about our previous connection years ago. White Diamond remembered vaguely, but I think she knew how much I wanted to become part of her staff to help other women the way I had been helped. I was hired in 2004 as an addiction counselor.

I love my work at Empowerment. What gets me up and going every single day is to suit up and show up. I never know who is going to walk through my door and allow me to reach out and touch them. I never know which broken woman's life I may make a difference in on any given day. Women helping women is what my job is all about. If I can save just one woman from going through life the way I did for so many years, I will have lived a full life.

My job is funded by a SAMSHA grant. The grant runs for five years. I am not sure what will become of my job when the five-year period is up, but I am neither worried nor afraid as I have learned to trust in God, and that all will be well. I have become quite good at my job, and even though I may be loud, I know I make a difference each day. I have participants who have learned to respect what I have to say to them because they know I have journeyed down their very same road. I try to listen with open ears and good heart so I can really hear what they have to say. I know that each woman is an individual who deserves my good listening skills. I also know when to tell it like it is and to call the women on their poor choices. It was only when I was held accountable that I was able to become a responsible person who had the power to make good life choices. I strive to be the most compassionate, open-minded counselor that I can be.

In May of 2007, I moved from my condo to my own house. It has a little backyard with green grass. I have a finished basement and a garage; I love my house; it is all mine. When I owned my condo, I thought I was something! But now that I own an actual house, I feel like I have died and gone to heaven. Life continues to treat me very well.

I would one day like to open my own agency for women. It would be a place where healing begins. It would be a place where women could get their lives back together. The goal would be for women helping women to do life well. The doors would always be open, but participants would need to work for the grocery vouchers and the bus token given to them. They could not just come with their hand out and not do anything for the help they would receive. It would be a place where women could heal at their own pace.

My philosophy would be based on the Bible; it would not be hard-core, only gentle influence on the women so they could learn to know God. I believe we all have a basic fundamental idea of who God is. I believe that God exists, and His strength comes from inside me. Also, God never closes the door on any of us. We are His children whom He adores and longs for us to succeed in life. I would not push any of my beliefs down anyone's throat; I only long to show others what I found and how God saved my life.

My agency would be one I would wish to run without all the bureaucracy. I think sometimes things just take too long and are far too complicated. All women ought to be free to be who each of us is meant to be without any strings attached. We each have different gifts and talents just waiting to be tapped into. We are all like the woman at the well who met Jesus one day, long ago. He told her everything she ever did and still loved her for who she was. In His acceptance of her as she was, she came to believe, and she brought others to believe too. He changed her whole life because He loved her and did not judge her. That is the role model on which I would build my agency.

I would name my agency the Coco Center after my beloved son. All Coco ever wanted for me was to get well. He taught me how to love and support those we care for without being judgmental. He tried so hard never to give up on me; my center would be my living testimony to Coco that he was right about me. I persevered and got it right in the end. I would want Coco to know that about me. I never gave up.

I would have an onsite day care so that the women would not have to worry about where their precious babies were while they worked on healing. I long for each mother to be a virtuous mother, a mother who loves and cares for her child. No matter how often we fail as a mother, we must never give up. Mothers need to care for and parent their children. They should never run away from their children, no matter how difficult and overwhelming life can become. I was given a second chance with Princess, and it is a gift and an opportunity I long to encourage every mother to take. Parenting classes, GED classes, life skills, drug and alcohol counseling, and job skills classes would be some of the types of programs I would like to offer. I would hope I could find counselors who were skilled in listening to each and every participant. Genuine listeners were the ones who helped me the most on my long journey back. They heard me, did not judge, were compassionate, and believed in me. They also held me accountable for my decisions and actions, but they showed me a new way of living life. They were genuine mentors.

I would need to go back to school and get my degree in human services as well as a degree in business management. It would be important to know how to manage the books and budget and write grants in order for me to be successful in running my own center. I love school and learning. I have developed enough good, strong self-esteem and confidence to know I could do these things even though I am entering my middle years of life. I am not afraid.

I want to embrace life for all it has to offer and know I have experiences I can offer to others. I have learned that it is okay to fall and fall again, but it is worth the risks in life to get back up each time and continue on life's way. I never gave up, and I have so many who never gave up on me. I am forever grateful that I have found God and know that He has shown me how good life can be without drugs and alcohol. It is a conscious daily choice that I choose to remain drug- and alcohol-free. I made it, even though it has taken me far longer than I had hoped. I think Coco would be proud to know his mama is well, and she is devoting the rest of her life to helping other women to be healthy and clean as well. I made it, Coco. I made it!

ABOUT THE AUTHOR

Rosalyn is a native of Denver, Colorado, who has a strong passion for helping people who have fallen asleep due to religious teachings. She is a mother and a grandmother of three, and she spends her time with music, dominoes, and cards when she isn't passionately writing. She aspires to one day attract the attention of the multitude in speaking of this awesome power that we all possess if we open our spirit, ears, and hearts. As a follower of the voice of God, she hopes that this writing helps others in understanding the truth that our universe is comprised of grace, love, peace, and gentleness.

CPSIA information can be obtained
at www.ICGtesting.com
Printed in the USA
FFHW022257221119
56114370-62206FF